「3・11」生命の記憶

未来へのメッセージ

創価学会東北青年部 編

第三文明社

景勝地として親しまれてきた「高田松原」。約7万本は津波によって流されたが、唯一残った一本は「奇跡の一本松」と呼ばれ、復興のシンボルとなった（2011年6月撮影、岩手県陸前高田市）

The 'miracle pine.' Before the tsunami, 70,000 pine trees lined the beach at scenic Takata Matsubara. This was the only one to survive. It has become a symbol of the town's restoration. (June 2011, Rikuzentakata City, Iwate Prefecture)

創価学会音楽隊による「希望の絆」コンサート。これまでに70回以上開催されている(2014年11月撮影、宮城県名取市)

"Building Bonds of Hope" series of concerts by the Soka Gakkai Music Corps. The Corps has held more than 70 concerts in the Tohoku region. (November 2014, Natori City, Miyagi Prefecture)

「3・11」生命(いのち)の記憶——未来へのメッセージ

発刊にあたって

東日本大震災から五年が経ちました。「3・11」という日は、一つの節目ではありますが、記念日でもなければ、目指す目標でもありません。

三月十一日は多くの方々の命が失われた「命日」であり、三月十二日は福島第一原発事故が起こったことで「避難がはじまった日」です。

そのことを語り、教えてくれたのが、被災された皆さんでした。

"あの日"、それまで築いてきた幸せな生活が否応(いやおう)なく奪われたこと。何度も引っ越しを重ねてなお、今も避難生活が続いていること。当事者から教えていただかなければ、わからない話が多くありました。

現在、被災地に赴くと、景色から震災の爪痕が見えなくなった街もあります。町全体がうねりをあげて造成している風景もあれば、いまだに人の住めない町もあります。

なんとなく日常を取り戻したように見えるだけに、一人一人の心が抱える傷は、ますます見えにくくなっています。

親や子どもを亡くした人もいれば、故郷を失った人もいます。被災者、避難者の方々がそれぞれ何を経験し、どんな思いで過ごしているのかをうかがい知ることは、容易でなくなってきています。

創価学会東北青年部は平和キャンペーン「SOKAグローバルアクション」の一環として、被災された方々への聞き取り活動を展開してきました。その模様は『3・11』生命の記憶──子どもたちへのメッセージ」と題して、月刊教育誌『灯台』に連載されております。

そしてこのたび、代表の方々の証言をまとめ、英訳も加えて、本書を発刊する運びとなりました。

震災当日に起こった出来事、当時の思いにつぶさに耳を傾けることは、同じ東北で暮らし、復興ボランティアに携わってきた青年部メンバーにとっても驚きが多く、「貴重な経験をすることができ、復興に果たすべき使命を新たにしました」との声もうかがいました。

また、今なお復興の途上にあるにもかかわらず、震災当時のことを語ってくださった皆さんからは、「人に話すことで気持ちの整理ができてよかった」「活字になったことで、子どもたちに教えられる」との感想も寄せられています。

こうした「経験の共有」の重要性は、二〇一五年三月に開催された国連防災世界会議の採択文書「仙台防災枠組」にも謳(うた)われるところとなりました。

記憶の風化と戦う術は、被災者が自ら語る言葉によるところが大きいと思います。それは同時に、どんな困難にも負けない人間の精神の力を語ることでもあります。

この千年に一度の大災害に遭っても、"心の財は壊されなかった"皆さんの体験を、私たち青年が未来に伝え残すことは、次世代への大きな財産になると確信します。

最後に、本書の出版にあたっては、第三文明社の皆さまをはじめ、多くの方にお世話になりました。心より御礼申し上げます。

二〇一六年三月

創価学会東北青年部

目次 「3・11」生命の記憶──未来へのメッセージ

発刊にあたって………3

第1章 岩手県

震災を機に、十四年の
引きこもりから息子が再起。
釜石市 杉田秀夫・強子………16

生徒たちの命を守った
日頃からの訓練と防災意識。
大船渡市 山本和孝………24

陸前高田の海に
再び勝利の大漁旗を！
陸前高田市 村上正彦・文子………32

第2章 宮城県

息子との約束を実現し、
バッティングセンターを建設。

気仙沼市
千葉清英 …… 44

世界的にも例がない大災害のなかで、
地域社会の"復興"に挑戦。

気仙沼市
松田 憲 …… 56

「がんばろう！石巻」の看板を設置。
「ど根性ひまわり」で世界に絆を広げる。

石巻市
黒澤健一 …… 66

第3章 福島県

避難指示の境界線近くで
暮らし続ける。

南相馬市
松本吉弘・優子 …… 80

第4章 救援活動をふり返る

東日本大震災と「励ましの絆」。

原発事故に負けず、避難先で店を再開。
郷里の人に元気を贈る。

飯舘村 赤石澤 榮・敏子 ……… 90

震災後の奮闘を支えた
笑顔のふれあいと仲間の絆。

広野町 金澤金治・清子 ……… 100

山根幹雄 ……… 110

写真：宍戸清孝（クレジットのない写真すべて）
　　　ボクダ茂（100ページ）

東日本大震災関連データ

▶発生時刻：2011年3月11日
　　　　　14時46分18秒
▶震源位置：北緯38度06.2分
　　　　　東経142度51.6分
　　　　　深さ24km
▶マグニチュード：9.0

(出典：気象庁)

岩手県
宮城県
震源
福島県
福島第一原子力発電所

〈被害状況〉
▶死　者　　　1万5,894人
▶行方不明　　　2,563人
▶負傷者　　　　6,152人

▶全壊家屋　　12万1,783戸
▶半壊家屋　　27万8,140戸

(出典：2016年1月8日発表、警察庁)

第1章
岩手県

岩手県の被害状況

（出典：2016年1月8日発表、警察庁）

〈人的被害〉

死　者　　　4,673人
行方不明　　1,124人
負傷者　　　　213人

〈建物被害〉

全　壊　　1万9,597戸
半　壊　　　6,571戸

震災を機に、十四年の引きこもりから息子が再起。

津波によって
自宅を流された
杉田さんだが、
震災をきっかけとして、
息子さんが
引きこもりから脱却。
「人のために役立ちたい」と、
福祉の仕事に従事している。

杉田秀夫さん
杉田強子さん

(岩手県釜石市)

自宅は跡形もなく流された

二〇〇九年三月、釜石港湾口防波堤が完成した。「世界最大水深」の巨大防波堤だった。しかし、東日本大震災によって引き起こされた津波の威力は凄まじく、防波堤は倒壊。市街地にも甚大な被害をもたらした。

強子 あの揺れがきたときは、私は夫と外出中でした。私は海育ちの〝浜っこ〟だから、津波の怖さは小さいころから聞いて育っていました。「大きな地震があったら、少しでも高いところに逃げるんだ」って。
　気になったのは息子（継夫さん）のこと。息子はずっと引きこもっていたから、こんな大きな地震でも、外に出て逃げないのではないかと思ったんです。もしかすると、家がつぶれて瓦礫の下敷きになっているかもしれないって。
　しかも、自宅は海から二十メートルくらいしか離れていない。だから、津波

がくる前に息子を救い出したいという気持ちばかり。急いで家に帰ったら、なんと息子が玄関に立っていたんです！

秀夫　三人で車に乗り込み、避難所を探しました。途中で忘れ物に気づいて取りに帰ろうとしたら、息子が「ダメだ！」って。その一言があったから助かった。

強子　多くの人は「釜石港には世界有数の巨大な防波堤があるから大丈夫だ」って思っていたんじゃないかね。「3・11」の数日前に地震があったときも、津波は四十センチくらいだったから、今回も大丈夫だという気持ちがあったと思う。過信だったね。とにかく、少しでも高いところに逃げなきゃいけない。

秀夫　一九六〇（昭和三十五）年のチリ津波は波がザブーンとくるイメージだったけど、今回はだんだん水嵩(みずかさ)が増えてくる感じだった。近くに住む友人は、最初黒い点みたいに見えたものが、バリバリと音を立てて近づいてきたと言って

いました。

津波によって、近所の知人・友人が八人ほど犠牲になりました。

強子 その日は多目的グラウンドで車中泊し、一夜明けて家に戻ろうとしたら、国道が封鎖されていて入れなかった。仕方なく裏道を歩いたんだけど、泥だらけで、足を取られて歩けない。

それでも、なんとか家の近所までたどりついた。でも、津波で町全体が削り取られて、自宅は影も形もなかった。言葉が出なかったね。

大槌町にある実家も流され、家とともに流された兄の遺体は四日後に見つかりました。結局、私たちは姉の家に避難しました。

秀夫 そんな状況のなか、友人がわざわざ山を越えて安否確認に来てくれてね。その後もお米や物資を持ってきてくれて励ましてくれた。本当にありがたかったね。

強子 くじけてられねえ。私たちが頑張らないでどうするって思いましたね。

「負けじ魂ここにあり」

強子　震災前、息子はご飯のときも部屋から出てこなかった。食事はお弁当箱に詰めて、部屋に持っていってたんです。

高校二年の夏休み前に「学校に行きたくない」と言って中退してから引きこもっていました。一時は居酒屋や弁当屋で働いたこともあるんだけど、人間関係がうまくいかなくて続かなかった。

引きこもりになって、十四年が経っていました。

秀夫　毎年、お正月に「今年こそ、息子が引きこもりから抜けられるように」と祈っていました。毎年「今年こそ」って、その繰り返し。支えになったのは「負けじ魂ここにあり」という言葉だった。雑誌に載っていたその言葉を切り抜いて、常に持ち歩いていました。

強子　私たちも悩んでいたけど、息子が一番苦しんでいたと思う。

継夫さん（中央）とともに　　　　©Seikyo Shimbun

そんな息子が、震災を機に引きこもりから抜け出せた。神奈川から応援に来ていた先輩とハローワークに行って、仕事を見つけて働き出したんです。今は運転免許も取って、子育て支援のNPO法人で働いています。

秀夫 先日も、自分でコツコツ貯めたお金で、中古車を購入しました。

　津波で家をなくしたことで、他の人たちと交わったのがよかったと思いますね。そしてなんといっても、いい先輩たちが激励に通ってくれたのが大きかった。ほんとに感謝です。

震災後、献身的に働く人々の姿に触れた継夫さんは、「何でもいい、みんなのように、人のために、何か役に立つことがしたい」と思うようになったと話す。その決意が、現在の仕事につながっている。

秀夫　四年七カ月間、仮設住宅に住んだあと、復興住宅への入居申し込みに当選して、二〇一五年四月から入ることができました。

強子　大事なものを失ったけど、今は幸せ。仮設住宅にいたころも、ご近所の方に恵まれたし、引っ越し先でも、皆さん温かく迎えてくれました。今回の震災を通して学んだのは、近隣・遠方を問わず、日頃から人間関係を築いておくことの大切さ。いざというとき、そのつながりが本当に大事だと思いました。

秀夫　家も財産も全部なくなったけど、「負けじ魂ここにあり」って言葉が励

みになりましたね。「一時は負けたような姿であったとしても、最後に勝てばよい」って。
切り抜いた記事は、津波にも流されず、今でも大事にしています。
町の復興は遅れているし、漁業もまだまだ。不安もあるし、これからも大変だけど、一人一人の心の復興こそ大事。全国の皆さんが応援してくれてるから、負けでたまっか！
輝く釜石の未来に向けて、〝唇に歌を、心に太陽を〞との思いで、希望の道を共々に一歩ずつ歩んでゆきます。

生徒たちの命を守った日頃からの訓練と防災意識。

小学校の教諭を務める山本さんは地震直後、迅速に避難を呼びかけ、生徒たちの命を守った。つらい経験をした人こそ幸せになってほしいと、今日も励ましの日々を送っている。

山本和孝(やまもとかずたか)さん

(岩手県大船渡市)

校舎は津波に飲み込まれた

　私が勤務していた小学校は、越喜来湾から二〇〇メートルほどの場所にありました。
　大きな揺れがきたのは、特別支援学級の授業を終え、職員室に戻ったときでした。校舎の脇にあるらせん階段が、建物から切り離されてしまうほどのひどい揺れでした。
　「津波がくるぞ。すぐ避難しろ！」という校長の指示に従って、私はすぐに二階に駆け上がり、教室を回って高台への避難を呼びかけました。じつは大震災の前年に、校舎から高台に直接避難できる陸橋を作っていたので、その橋を渡って、子どもたちを迅速に避難させました。
　この地域は、昭和三陸地震（一九三三年）やチリ地震（一九六〇年）による津波など、何度も大きな被害を受けてきましたので、沿岸部にある学校の多くは

山本和孝

毎年避難訓練をしていました。私の学校も三月一日に避難訓練をしたばかりだったんです。

しかも震災二日前の三月九日に、三陸沖を震源とした大きめの地震があり、六十センチほどの津波があったばかりで、そのときも避難していました。そうした経験があったので、子どもたちも大きく動揺することなく、冷静に対処できたのだと思います。

山本さんたちの避難誘導によって、七十三人の生徒と教職員は全員無事だった。この経験を通し、いつ起こるかわからない災害への第一の備えは、「日常的な訓練だ」と山本さんは語る。

地震後三十分ほどで津波がきました。第一波は校庭にあった車が浮く程度でしたが、第一波が引きはじめたときに十五メートルもある真っ黒な第二波が

やってきて、三階建ての校舎を全部飲み込んでいきました。
その光景を見ながら、高台に避難してよかったと思うとともに、これが夜中だったり、学校が休みの日だったりすれば、子どもたちにもっと大きな被害が出ていたかもしれないと感じ、ゾッとしました。
その日は高台の公民館で、子どもたちと一緒に夜を明かしました。家族や友人たちのことも心配でしたが、その場を離れるわけにはいきません。明かりもつかず、電話もつながらない状況でしたが、ともかく、子どもたちの命を守らなければいけないという一心でした。

亡くなった友の分も生きる

私が勤務していた小学校は、もともと二〇一二年に近隣の二校と統合される予定だったのですが、震災のために前倒しして、震災の年に統合されました。

山本和孝

急な統合だったので、最初の年は校長が三人、副校長も三人いて、校歌も平等に一番ずつ歌いました（笑）。

慣れない環境で、子どもたちも大変だったと思います。

私が担当していた特別支援学級は教室もなくて、二年間、コンテナで授業を行いました。

そんななかでも、子どもたちの成長を実感できる嬉しい出来事もありました。大船渡には、子どもたちが物語を創作する「さんりく・おおふなとお話大賞」というコンクールがあるのですが、そこで、わが校の五年生の女子生徒が最優秀賞を受賞したのです。

ヤドカリを主人公にして津波のことを書いたその作文では、ヤドカリに「自分勝手だった人間が、震災後、励まし合っている。人間も捨てたものじゃない」と語らせていました。

じつはその子は、大好きだったおばさんを津波で亡くしていました。一時は

大船渡市の風景（2014年1月撮影）

ショックのために眠れなくなるなど、ひどく落ち込んでいましたが、多くの人から励ましを受けるなかで立ち直り、人々との絆の大切さを感じてくれたのです。

「3・11」を経験し、大変な思いをしたからこそ、子どもたちには成長してほしいし、幸せになってほしいと思っています。

また、これまで以上に地域に貢献する意識を持ってほしいと願っています。大人になって東北のために貢献できる人材に成長してくれたら、これほど嬉

山本和孝

しいことはありませんね。

山本さんは亡くなった知人・友人のためにも頑張っていこうと決意し、周囲の被災者一人一人を励まし続けてきた。

毎週のように仮設住宅などを訪問して、被災した方々の悩みをうかがっていますが、時とともに悩んでいる内容が変化しているのを感じます。将来に対する不安も大きいのだと思います。

復興への道には大きな困難が立ちはだかっていますが、地域の人たちと団結し、絆を強め合って、一歩一歩、歩みを運んでいきたいと決意しています。

亡くなられた方のことを思うと、今も悲しくて言葉になりません。「どうしてこんなことが……」という悔しさも拭えません。

しかし、だからこそ、そうした人たちのことは、十年経っても、二十年経っ

30

ても、絶対に忘れません。残された私たちは、その方たちの分まで、生きて生きて生き抜いて、使命を果たしていかなくてはいけないと強く思っています。

山本和孝

陸前高田の海に再び勝利の大漁旗を！

村上さんは長年漁業を営み、三陸ワカメ、ほたて、岩ガキの養殖をしてきた。
大震災のあと海を離れた漁師仲間もいるが、村上さんは新しい漁船を購入し、再び海に戻ってきた。

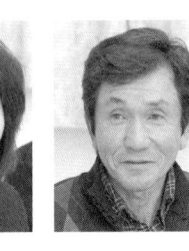

村上正彦さん
村上文子さん 

（岩手県陸前高田市）

思い出したくない光景

文子　地震が起きたとき、私は自宅にいました。台所で漬物を切っていたら、突然大きな揺れに襲われたんです。ストーブの上のヤカンがひっくり返るほどの大きな揺れで、しかも長く続きました。私は包丁を持ったまま、慌てて外に飛び出しました。

正彦　私はその日、沖合で養殖ワカメの収穫作業をしていたんですが、ワカメの刈り取りを終えて、港にある作業場に戻ってきたときに地震に遭いました。とっさに「津波がくる」と思ったので、買ったばかりのフォークリフトを高台に上げました。それから漁師仲間の一人が船を陸に引き上げようとしているのを手伝ったんですが、停電で機械が動かない。それで結局、引き上げることができませんでした。
　そうこうしていると、潮がどんどん引いていくのが見えました。深いところ

でも底が見えるくらい引いていった。不気味でしたよ。

「これは大変だ」と思って、すぐに高台にある自宅へ逃げました。結局、買ったばかりの船もリフト機も引き波にさらわれてしまいました。

揺れてから四十分ほどすると津波が押し寄せてきて、

文子　うちは高台だったから、町が津波に飲み込まれる様子が見えました。二階建ての家が崩れることなく、そのまま浮いたように流されていきました。

正彦　自分ももしあのとき、すぐに逃げなかったら、津波に飲み込まれていたかもしれません。

やっぱり、"津波てんでんこ"が大事。自分の命は自分で守る。妻は妻で逃げるし、俺は俺で逃げる。それぞれがバラバラに高台に向かって一目散(いちもくさん)に逃げなきゃいけない。大事なものを取りに戻ったり、誰かを探しに行ったりして、犠牲(ぎせい)になった人も多かった。

文子　何がつらいって、昨日まで元気だった知り合いがたくさん亡くなったこ

34

とが一番つらかった。あまりのショックで、自分自身も死にそうでした。「破壊は一瞬」っていうけど、頑張って積み上げてきたものが、本当に一瞬にして崩れ去ってしまった。

正彦　復興のためには、忘れることも大事。あの日のことを忘れられなくて、そこから抜け出せない人もいますから。

忘れられないけど、二度と思い出したくない光景です。

陸前高田市では市の人口の七・二％にあたる約千七百人が津波の犠牲となった（行方不明者含む）。生き残った人たちの前にも、再建に向けた厳しい現実が待っていた。

正彦　家が大丈夫だったから、当面の食料はなんとかなったけれど、自分たちが食べるものがなくなった（笑）。近所に全部あげてしまって、

文子　ご近所さんは津波で家もなくなって、着の身着のままで避難していたので、「なんとかしてあげなきゃ」って。気がついたら、水揚げしたワカメもお米も全部あげていました（笑）。

正彦　停電は二カ月くらい続きました。水もこなくて、近くの川からバケツで運んで、お湯を沸かしたり、頭を洗ったりしていました。少しでもみんなに食べてもらって、胃袋を元気にしたいという気持ちでした。

文子　暗いなかで食事すると、何を食べているかわからなくて、おいしくなかったですね。

全国からの支援に励まされて

正彦　震災のあとは毎日、漁港に散乱した瓦礫の撤去をしていました。それをしないと漁にも出られないし、次の養殖もできないから。

36

文子　震災から三日経ったころに、自衛隊による救援物資が届きました。本当にありがたかった。当時の活動の様子を映像で見ると、今でも涙が出そうになります。

正彦　全国の創価学会の皆さんにも本当に助けられました。北海道や青森をはじめ、たくさんの方が支援に来てくれました。

文子　うちは犬を飼っていたんですが、犬に与えるエサがなくてとても苦労しました。それを知った学会の方が、わざわざ五十キロほど離れた遠野まで行って買ってきてくれたんです。また、「励ます言葉がないから」と言って、ハーモニカを吹いてくれた青年もいました。

正彦　震災後、兵庫のメンバーが三回も励ましに来てくれたことも忘れられません。「自分たちも阪神淡路大震災で大変な目に遭ったんで、じっとしていられなかった」って。

文子　その後、兵庫に招待されて、交流の集いに参加しました。それまでは瓦

37　村上正彦・文子

礫の山しか見ない生活だったから、明るい会場で皆さんの笑顔に触れて、本当に心が前向きになりました。

正彦 震災をきっかけに知り合った東京・町田市のある小学校からは、「本物の大漁旗（たいりょうばた）を子どもたちに見せたい」という要望があったんです。そこで、私たちの船・栄光丸（えいこうまる）の大漁旗を貸してあげましたね。

文子 私たちの船は沈んでしまったけど、大漁旗だけは残りました。さらにその後、子どもたちが大漁旗を手作りして、わざわざ持参してくれました。漁旗を使った運動会の様子をビデオに収めて送ってくれました。本当に嬉（うれ）しいプレゼントでした。

　震災を機に、海を離れた漁師仲間もいるという。村上さんも一時は漁師を辞めることを考えた。それでも、新しい漁船「第三栄光丸」を購入し、再び海に戻ってきた。

苦悩を乗り越え、再び海に戻った村上さん夫妻
©Seikyo Shimbun

正彦 私が漁師をはじめた二十五年ほど前は漁師仲間が二十八人いたけど、今は六人しかいない。

年齢の問題もあるとは思うけど、船は沈んだし、海の下にどれだけの瓦礫があるかもわからない。海が怖いと言って、辞めた人も多い。

文子 あの津波を見てしまったら、怖くて、漁師を辞めたいと思うのが普通かもしれません。震災後、一度も漁に出ず、港に停泊している船もありますから。漁を再開した人でも、いろんな葛藤はまだあると思う。

正彦　私も辞めることを考えました。辞めるほうがかえって楽だと思った。辞めるか、進むか、ずいぶん悩んだけど、結局は「進むしかない！」って決めました。
　私が戻ったのは、漁師には魅力がいっぱいあるから。頑張ったらその分だけ稼（かせ）げるし、おいしいものを食べられるから（笑）。獲（と）れたてのウニやアワビはうまいよ。漁師の仕事って最高だと思う。

文子　いろんな人たちから、「村上さんのおいしいワカメ、また食べたいな」と言ってもらえるからね。大きな力になりますよ。

正彦　ついこのあいだも、アワビが六十一キロも獲れた。開港一番の大漁（笑）。二桁獲れれば万々歳（ばんばんざい）だから、六十一キロってすごいんだ。ワカメの収穫も断トツだった。

文子　大変な状況だけど、やっぱり人生勝利の姿を示したいからね。「負けてたまっか」って、毎日悔いなく生きていきたいと思っています。

40

第2章
宮城県

宮城県の被害状況
(出典：2016年1月8日発表、警察庁)

〈人的被害〉
死　者　　9,541人
行方不明　1,237人
負傷者　　4,145人

〈建物被害〉
全　壊　　8万2,999戸
半　壊　　15万5,129戸

| 秋田県 | 岩手県 |

気仙沼市

南三陸町

登米市

石巻市

女川町

東松島市

仙台市

太平洋

福島県

息子との約束を実現し、バッティングセンターを建設。

津波によって家族七人を
亡くした千葉さんは、
小学生の長男と二人で
震災後の絶望を乗り越えてきた。
親子で約束した
「バッティングセンター建設」の
夢を実現し、復興に向けて
希望の前進を続けている。

千葉清英(ちばきよひで)さん

(宮城県気仙沼市)

橋の欄干につかまり九死に一生

あの日は、家族で営む牛乳販売店の店舗で地震に遭いました。学校へ行っていた息子（当時・小学三年生）と私を除く家族七人を、二台の車に乗せて高台にある自宅へ避難させました。

しばらくすると、真っ黒い津波が迫ってくるのが見えました。慌てて二階に上がったものの、そこに津波がきたんです。無我夢中で屋根の上に飛び移りましたが、その瞬間に建物が浮き上がりはじめました。私は屋根にしがみついたまま、なすがまま流れに翻弄されました。やがて屋根がギシギシと建物から剥がされていき、私は黒い波の中に放り出されたのです。その瞬間、「終わった」と思いました。

それでも、なんとか浮き上がろうと瓦礫につかまっては沈み、また別の瓦礫

千葉清英

にっかまっては沈むということを何度も繰り返しました。着ていたダウンジャケットは水を吸い込んで重くなり、腕が上がらなかったので脱ぎ捨てました。小さな瓦礫では沈んでしまうので、大きな瓦礫にしがみついて沈まないようになんとかこらえていると、津波のあとの引き波がきました。このままでは海まで流されます。引き波にさらわれ、橋にぶつかりそうになったその瞬間、とっさに橋の欄干に腕を突っ込んでしがみつき、九死に一生を得ることができたのです。

その後、なんとか橋の上によじ登りましたが、日が暮れて、ともかく寒い。足も裸足です。雪も降ってきました。のちに、あばら骨が三本折れていたことがわかりましたが、そのときは、あまりの寒さに痛みは感じませんでした。少しでも暖をとろうと、流されてきた発砲スチロールを棒で手繰り寄せて、それを粉々にして体に突っ込みました。

寝たら死ぬと思い、震えながら大声を出したり、叫んだりしましたが、その

まま気を失ってしまい、目が覚めたら朝になっていました。
「ああ、生きていたな」というのがそのときの実感でした。と同時に、「すべてが夢であってほしい」と願いました。しかし、体に積もった雪を払って身を起こすと、目の前には想像を絶する惨状が広がっていました。
避難所に向かう途中、花屋さんでぬるま湯に砂糖を溶かしたものを飲ませてもらいましたが、あのときのおいしさ、ありがたさは忘れられません。

地震発生時に小学校にいた長男は無事に避難しており、震災から三日後に、千葉さんと再会することができた。しかし、車二台で避難した家族七人の安否は、その後もわからなかった。

警察から連絡があり、家族の死亡を知らされたのは三週間後のことでした。妻と二人の幼い娘、義父母と義妹、遺体安置所に行くと七人が並んでいました。

千葉清英

そして甥っ子の七人です。みんな、車の中で亡くなっていたそうです。
遺体を見た瞬間は腰から崩れ落ちましたが、「泣いている余裕などない」というのが正直な気持ちでした。目の前には震災後の厳しい現実があったからです。

息子にはしばらくの間、家族の死を伝えることができませんでした。息子が待つ避難所へ帰るたびに、「今日もダメだった」「まだ見つからない」と嘘をつき続けました。その一方で、一緒にお風呂に入ったときなどに、「もう無理かもしれない」「もう会えないよ」と、心の準備ができるように少しずつ話していきました。

息子に本当のことを言えたのは、葬儀の三日前のことです。
遺体との対面はあまりにも残酷だと思ったので、息子に「いい思い出にしよう」と言うと、息子は涙をじっとこらえて、「そう」とだけ言いました。
息子が初めて涙を見せたのは、火葬場に行ったときでした。そこで初めて、

息子は声を上げて号泣しました。

しかし、それで吹っ切れたのか、その後は弔問客に挨拶したり、誘導したりするなど、気丈に振る舞っていました。

その後も亡くなった家族のことを一切話さないので、「本当に忘れてしまったんじゃないか」とこちらが心配になるほどでしたが、息子なりに私に気を使ってくれていたのでしょう。

バッティングセンターの建設を約束

四十九日忌法要を終え、千葉さんは牛乳販売店の再建に取り組んだ。ゼロからの再出発だった。そんななか、長男を励まそうと、千葉さんはバッティングセンターを作ることを決意する。

私自身、中学・高校と野球をやっていましたし、息子もリトルリーグに入っていて、野球が大好きだったので、震災後は毎日二人でキャッチボールをしていました。

ある日、仕事の合間に、岩手県奥州市のバッティングセンターに息子と立ち寄ったんです。そこで、息子が汗をかきながら無心でボールを打っている姿を見て、「これだ！」と思いました。

その後も月に一回程度、車で一時間半かけて、同じバッティングセンターに息子を連れていきました。そんなある日の帰り道、息子がふと「気仙沼にバッティングセンターがあったらいいのに。お父さん作ってよ」と言ったんです。

「気仙沼には、やりたくてもできない仲間がいっぱいいるんだ」って。そのとき私は、軽い気持ちで「よし、わかった」と答えました。ピッチングマシンを一台購入して、空き地にネットを設置すれば、すぐにできると思ったんです。

しかし、日々の忙しさに追われてその約束をすっかり忘れていたころ、息子

50

「お父さん、いつ建ててくれるの？」と聞いてきたのです。私は「こいつ本気だったんだ」と思いました。彼が頼れるのは私しかいないわけです。「この約束を破ったら、息子の人生がどうなってしまうかわからないし、私自身が絶対に後悔する」と感じて、スイッチが入りました。「気仙沼にバッティングセンターを作ろう！」と。

しかし、決意はしたものの、資金や建設用地のめどはまったく立っていませんでした。とにかく牛乳販売の仕事を頑張るしかないと思い、オリジナル商品を作ることを決めました。試行錯誤の末に生まれたのが「希望ののむヨーグルト」です。「気仙沼に希望を！」という思いで付けた名前です。

その利益でバッティングセンターを建設しようと考えていましたが、すぐにその資金が集まったわけではありません。物産展をやったり、全国で行われているさまざまな復興イベントに出かけたりして、ヨーグルトを売って歩きました。その活動をテレビや新聞などで取り上げていただき、次第に全国から注文がく

51 千葉清英

るようになったのです。

バッティングセンターの建設に向けて、さまざまな応援もいただきました。ゴルフの打ちっぱなし練習場を経営している方が「近々店を閉めるから、よかったらうちのネットと支柱を使ってくれ」と申し出てくださったり、茨城県の土建業者さんが「造成に使う土なら、ダンプでいくらでも運んであげるよ」と連絡くださったり、土地もお貸しいただけることになりました。そうした全国の皆さまからの応援のおかげで、ついに建設のめどが立ったのです。

バッティングセンターは二〇一四年三月三十日にオープンしました。名前は「気仙沼フェニックス」です。「気仙沼が不死鳥のように蘇るように」との願いを込めて名付けました。また、バッティングセンターの打席数は七席で、亡くなった家族と同じ数を設置しました。

千葉さんは部屋の壁に、「厳しい冬を乗り越えれば、必ず暖かい春が待って

52

いる！ だから、絶対に諦(あきら)めない！ 絶対に負けない！」と貼り出した。現実の厳しさに負けそうなとき、何度もこの言葉を見つめ、口にして、歩み続けてきた。

バッティングセンターのオープンの日に思いきりバットを振る長男・瑛太さん

家族を失ってから、私のなかには常に、"泣いている自分"と"懸命に動いている自分"の、二人の自分がいました。そんななかで、「きっと、亡くなった家族は"幸せになってほしい"と思っているはずだ」と素直に思えたのです。
自分に何を望んでいるだろうか」と考え、「亡くなった私たちに"幸せになってほしい"と思っているはずだ」と素直に思えたのです。
そのときから私は泣くのをやめて、「これからは人のために動き、働こう」と腹を決めることができました。そう思えたときが、私にとって希望が生まれた瞬間でした。

町の復興とともに"心の復興"の大切さが叫ばれていますが、"心の復興"とは"新しい自分"を探すことではないでしょうか。たんに震災前に戻るのは"復旧"であって"復興"ではない。"新しい自分"を見つけ出すことができたときが"心の復興"であり、そのとき希望や夢を持てるようになるんだろうと思います。

私はこれからバッティングセンターを通して、気仙沼に多くの"夢"を届けたいと思っています。また十年後には、自分の出身地である東京の調布市と気仙沼市を姉妹都市にしたいという夢も持っています。
そして何より、ただ一人残った家族である息子の"人生の道しるべ"になりたいと思っています。どんなに困難な状況にあっても、負けじ魂を胸に大きな夢に向かって走っていく──そんな姿こそ、子どもたちに見せるべき大人の姿だと思うのです。

千葉清英

世界的にも例がない大災害のなかで、地域社会の"復興"に挑戦。

松田さんは
中東やアフリカ、アジア諸国で
難民・国内避難民の支援などに
携（たずさ）わってきた。
東日本大震災以後は、
被災地・気仙沼（けせんぬま）市に移住し、
地域の復興と発展に
取り組んでいる。

松田（まつだ） 憲（けん）さん

（宮城県気仙沼市）

インドネシアのテレビで見た震災のニュース

私が海外での人道支援活動をはじめたのは、幼少期に母方の祖父の戦争体験を聞いたことが潜在的なきっかけになっているかもしれません。戦争の恐ろしさにショックを受け、心の中に平和を重んじる気持ちが刻まれたのだと思います。

その後、一般企業に勤め、支援活動とは無関係に生きてきましたが、二〇〇一年の「9・11」アメリカ同時多発テロのニュースをテレビで見たとき、「ニューヨークでボランティア活動をしたい」との思いが込み上げてきたんです。突き動かされるように、さまざまな国際協力団体に連絡をした結果、アフガニスタンへ物資を運搬する活動に携わることになりました。

ニューヨークに行くつもりだったのがアフガニスタンになり、二週間程度の予定が四カ月になるなど、当初の希望とは異なりましたが、そのときの活動が

57　松田憲

きっかけとなって、私はそれ以後、さまざまな国際協力団体に所属しながら、紛争地や大規模災害現場での支援事業に取り組むようになりました。

二〇一一年に東日本大震災が発生したときは、東ティモールでの活動から戻る途中でした。インドネシアの食堂のテレビで、初めて震災のニュースを見たんです。「とんでもないことが起きてしまった」と思い、一刻も早く被災地に入りたいと、すぐに帰国の手配をしました。

それまでの経験から、有事の際に人と同じ行動をすると足止めされて動けなくなるとわかっていましたので、別のルートを考えました。

インドネシアから帰国する場合、普通は成田空港に向かうのですが、関西国際空港から入りました。大阪から新幹線で東京方面に向かう際も、大きな駅を利用すると足止めされると予想して、静岡県の掛川駅で降り、車をレンタルして栃木県に向かいました。そこにヘリコプターを借りられるところがあったからです。

58

ヘリコプターで向かう目的地は宮城県気仙沼市にしました。その理由の一つは、ヘリコプターの燃料の問題です。これ以上進んだら戻れないという最北の地まで行こうと思いました。

もう一つの理由は、気仙沼は支援が滞りそうな場所だったからです。東北には新幹線と東北道が"背骨"のように走っています。陸路からの支援が中心になるとすると、新幹線や東北道からアクセスしやすい地域は支援してくださる方が早く到着する可能性が高いと考えました。

そこで、一緒に行動したチーム内で話し合い、緊急時に陸路でのアクセスがどうしても困難となってしまう沿岸部で、人口も経済規模も大きい気仙沼市に着陸することにしたのです。

松田さんがインドネシアから帰国し、被災地に入ったのは震災翌日の三月十二日のことだった。首都圏で"帰宅難民"が発生するなど国内が騒然とするな

59 松田 憲

かでの、迅速(じんそく)な行動だった。

"支援者"ではなく"パートナー"として連携

　気仙沼に入ってからは、それまでの経験を生かして手を打っていきました。三日後に何が必要になるか、一週間後、一カ月後にどういったニーズがあるかといったことを、ある程度予測しながら物資の手配をしました。
　しかし、中・長期的な視野に立っての復興は本当に難しいと痛感させられました。先進国で、しかも高齢化が進んだ地域で、これほど大きな災害を経験したことは、世界的にも例がありません。誰も経験したことがない事態なので"答え"がないのです。ですから、手探りのなかで必死に進んでいくという毎日でした。
　中・長期的な支援で大切なことは、やはり課題の解決に向けて、地域の人た

60

ちと一緒に考えて行動することだと思います。そのためには、〝支援者〟という立場よりも、地域社会とタッグを組む〝パートナー〟として携わっていくことが大事だと感じました。

そこで私たちは、気仙沼に「pensea（ペンシー）」という会社を立ち上げました。宮城県や岩手県の農林水産業の生産者さんや水産加工会社さんとチームを組み、私たちがデザインやマーケティングなどをサポートすることで、地域産業の魅力を広くお伝えしたいと考えたのです。

たとえば、水産加工会社を再建しても、販路がないという現状があります。震災前は加工品をスーパーに卸していた会社が多かったのですが、震災によって商品を供給できなくなったために、スーパーの側は仕入れ先を変更せざるをえなくなりました。その結果、加工会社がせっかく工場を再建しても、販路がなくなっていたのです。そこで、私たちは水産加工会社と一緒にオンラインショップを立ち上げ、新しいブランドを作って直接販売をはじめました。

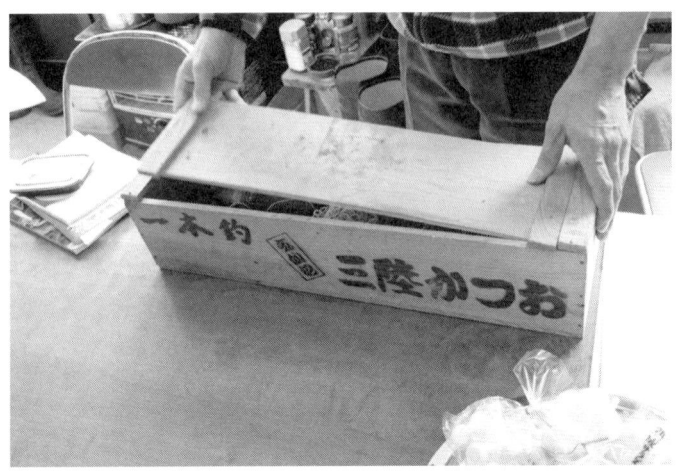

「pensea」では東北の海の豊かさ、美しさを伝える商品の販売など、さまざまな取り組みを行っている
(写真提供：pensea & Co.)

そうした取り組みをしていくうえで課題の一つになったのは、経営陣の世代間意識の違いだったように思います。現役の社長さんたちは七十代の方が多く、二十代、三十代の次の世代の方たちが新しいチャレンジを考えても、「これまでの自分の経験を生かして再建する」と考えていらっしゃる。しかも、社長さんたちは激動の時代を生き抜いてきた百戦錬磨の方々ですので、その勘には鋭いものがあります。

そのようななかで新規事業を立ち上げるには、さまざまな調整が必要でした。そこで、私たちが経営チームの一員となり、彼らの手足や頭脳となって、一緒にチャレンジをしたわけです。

今は地域経済を担っていく人と〝伴走〟して、いかにいいものを作り、広めていくかに挑戦しています。

海外と東北での支援活動を経験し、松田さんはあらためて日本の特色や東北

63　松田 憲

人の強さに気づいたと話す。

日本には優秀な人材が多く、意識も高い。インフラも整っています。私たちのような国際協力団体にかぎらず、行政やボランティアグループ、民間企業のサポートの質も、どんどん高まっています。

ただし、日本は高齢化が進んでおり、青年が減少しています。そこは課題だと思います。

途上国はセーフティネットやインフラも整っておらず、厳しい状況にあります。しかし、若者が多い。劣悪(れつあく)な環境にもかかわらず、子どもたちの瞳(ひとみ)は輝いています。そこに未来を感じます。

もちろん、東北の被災地でも、元気な子どもたちと数多く出会いました。つらい避難生活のなかでの楽しい出来事を語ってくれる子どもがいました。大人たちが頑張ってくれていることへの感謝を話す子どももいました。そうしたプ

64

ラスの思い出を少しでも多く記憶して、それを自分自身の成長や使命感につなげていってもらいたいと思います。

震災から五年を迎える二〇一六年からは、地域の生産者の方とともに作り上げてきた商品やサービスを海外に発信できるように、現在新しいプロジェクトも進めています。具体的には、海外のクリエイターさんとのネットワークづくりや、海外での東北産品の販売、海外からの旅行客の皆さんに東北に来ていただけるような情報発信です。まずは、三月にハワイでのお祭りに出店し紹介していきたいと考えています。

震災直後から、世界中の方々のご支援のおかげで、東北の皆さんはここまで進んでくることができました。それをご報告し、また感謝の思いをお伝えするべく、世界への発信に取り組んでいきたいと考えています。

松田 憲

「がんばろう！石巻」の看板を設置。
「ど根性ひまわり」で世界に絆を広げる。

黒澤健一さん

黒澤さんが自宅の跡地に立てた「がんばろう！石巻(いしのまき)」の看板は、復興のシンボルとなっている。さらに看板の脇から発芽(はつが)した「ど根性ひまわり」が、震災を忘れない〝使者〟として世界に広がっている。

(宮城県石巻市)

松の木につかまり一晩過ごす

　その日、私は石巻市の隣の東松島市にいました。恐怖を感じるほどの大きな揺(ゆ)れが続き、向かいの建物がまるで豆腐のようにグラグラ揺れて、こちらに倒れてくるのではないかと思うほどでした。

　揺れが収まると、私は自宅（兼店舗）に戻ろうと思いました。配管業を営んでいますので、「こんなに大きな地震なら、ライフラインの確保が必要になる」と思い、とにかく何かの役に立てればと考えたのです。

　車で自宅に向かう途中、外出していた妻から「自宅に戻る」と電話が入り、私も「わかった。俺も戻るから」と伝えたのですが、その後すぐに津波警報が発せられました。「逃げなきゃダメだ」と伝えようと思い、何度も妻に電話しましたが、つながりません。

　「ともかく行くしかない！」と思い、私はそのまま自宅に向かいました。

67　黒澤健一

反対車線は避難する車で大渋滞していましたが、私は海岸線を自宅に向かってひた走りました。すると、道の前方にバリケードのようなものが見えてきたのです。「立ち入り禁止か？」と思ってよく見てみたら、それは津波で流されてきた車でした。慌ててUターンをして逃げましたが、今度は反対側からも津波が押し寄せ、挟み撃ちになってしまいました。

「このままではダメだ」と、私は車を捨てて木に登りました。しかし、その木は枝が細くて折れてしまい、頭から落下。再び土手に駆け上がり松の木にジャンプし、必死になってよじ登りました。すぐ下を津波が凄い勢いで流れてきて、どんどん水嵩も増してきました。

街路樹や自動車も流されてきました。私と同じように木にしがみついている人もいましたが、しばらくすると姿が消えていました。たぶん流されてしまったと気づきました。

その後、一度だけ妻と電話が通じたのですが、妻は「自宅にいる」とだけ話

すと電波が悪くなり、話の途中で電話は切れてしまいました。
雪が降ってきて、どんどん暗くなってきました。暗闇のなか、助けを求める声やうめき声が遠くから聞こえてきましたが、どうすることもできませんでした。その日は松の木にしがみついて一晩を過ごしました。

朝、木から降りて、私は自宅に向かって歩きはじめました。昨日まで建ち並んでいた家はなくなり、どこもかしこも水没していて、まるで湖のようでした。膝まで水につかりながら、ともかく自宅を目指しました。水の中は見えませんから、側溝やマンホールに足を取られながら歩きました。

自宅の方角を見ると、その周辺は曇っているように見えました。しかしそれは火災の煙だったのです。妻の名前を叫びながらヘドロの水の中を歩きました。上空を旋回するヘリコプターの音がうるさく、私の声はかき消されました。

悔しくて悔しくて、たまりませんでした。

火災のせいで自宅にはたどりつけません。「ああ、ダメだ。妻はもうダメか

69　　黒澤健一

もしれない」と、涙が止まりませんでした。

それでも、あきらめきれず、一日中探し続けた末、日和山の避難所で妻と再会できました。妻の姿を見たとき、私は腰が抜けたようにその場にしゃがみこみ、言葉も出ませんでした。

黒澤夫人の話によると、津波に流された家が突っ込んできたため、黒澤さんの自宅は大破。壁も屋根も壊され、半分残った二階の部屋で、まるで海の中に立っているような状態のところを、日没寸前に救出されたという。

「がんばろう！石巻」の看板を創る

震災後、みんなうつむいたまま、家の痕跡や行方不明の家族を探していました。遺体の捜索もはじまり、毛布に包まれたご遺体が並んでいました。あるべ

きものがなくなって、いるべき人がいなくなって、絶望しかありませんでした。
私は、その光景を見たとき「なんとかしなきゃいけない」「生き残った自分にできることは何だ」と考えました。
ちょうど自宅の跡地は道路に面していて、避難所のある日和山からもよく見える場所なので、皆さんの希望になる看板を創ろうと思いました。
看板は流されたベニヤ板などを集めて、知り合いの大工さんに頼みました。
「がんばろう！石巻」の文字は、友人と三人で書きました。「石巻」の字を水色にしたのは、津波があったとしても、やはり石巻は海の町だと思ったからです。

震災からわずか一カ月。廃材や瓦礫を再利用して作られた縦一・八メートル、横十・八メートルの大看板は、多くのメディアで取り上げられ、復興のシンボルとして世界からも注目を集めた。

71　黒澤健一

看板を書く黒澤さんたち（2011年4月11日／写真提供：毎日新聞社）

次第に看板前に花を手向ける光景を目にするようになりました。最初は違和感を覚えましたが、この震災でひときわ多くの人的被害を出したのがこの宮城県石巻市です。

亡くなられた方々を思う気持ちが、ここを、そのような場にしたのだと思います。

じつは、看板を立てる前には、心の葛藤がありました。食べるものにも困っている大変なときに、こんな看板を立てていいのか、と。

でも、看板を書いている途中に、近

所のおじさんが「おお、頑張ってるな！　俺も頑張るからな！」って言ってくれて、この看板には力があるな、と思えました。

看板の「がんばろう！」という言葉に、今も心が苦しくなるという人もいます。自分の覚悟として、そうした思いの方々とも向き合いながら、この場所で日々を重ねていきたいと思っています。

「ど根性ひまわり」を"伝承の使者"に

瓦礫しかなく、色がなくなった町に少しでも色を取り戻したいと思い、看板の周囲に花の苗を植えました。

ある日、花の水やりと周辺の草取りをしていると、妻が「がんばろう！石巻」の看板の横に食い込む形で発芽しているひまわりを見つけました。津波で種が自然に流れ着いたのでしょうか。手を加えて様子をみると芽はぐんぐん成

黒澤健一

長して、見事にひまわりの花を咲かせました。
驚きました。この辺りは流れ込んだヘドロの悪影響で、夏になっても雑草すらほとんど生えない地域でした。草花が育つこと自体が不思議な場所にひまわりが咲いたのです。

震災から数カ月経ち、復旧で心も体も疲れがピークの時期でした。そうしたなか、このひまわりを見つけ、塩害にも負けず成長する姿に、「ひまわりが頑張っているのに、自分が頑張らないわけにはいかない」と、希望をもらいました。

私はひまわりを「ど根性ひまわり」と名付け、SNSを使ってひまわりの開花を発信しました。すると、多くの人々がその情報を喜んでくれたのです。

黒澤さんは「ど根性ひまわり」の種を十粒ずつ袋に入れ、お世話になった方々などにプレゼントした。すると、多くの方がそれぞれの地域で喜んで育て

74

はじめた。黒澤さんはその姿に、「ど根性ひまわり」の力を感じたという。

　私は「ど根性ひまわり」を未来に伝えていくために、一世、二世、三世と名付けて育てました。これは、たとえば、「ど根性ひまわり」が五十世になったとき、そのときの子どもたちが「なんで五十世なの？」と疑問に思って尋ねてくれれば、「これは東日本大震災のときにね……」と話すことができると思ったからです。「ど根性ひまわり」が、未来の子どもたちに震災のことや自然災害のことを学ぶ〝伝承の使者〟となるのです。

　現在、「ど根性ひまわり」六世の種が採れました。これからも七世、八世と育て、時を刻んでいきます。

　多くの方々の協力もあり、「ど根性ひまわり」は日本はもとより、インド、中国、アメリカ、イギリス、ブラジル、フランス、イタリアなど、世界中に広がり、希望と友情を育みながら、未来への旅を続けています。

75　黒澤健一

私は現在、「がんばろう！石巻の会」という市民グループを立ち上げ、活動しています。そこでは、「がんばろう！石巻」看板での市民の追悼行事や子どもたちへの語り部伝承活動、そして「ど根性ひまわり」を通じて震災のことを世界に広め、未来に伝承する活動をしています。

これからも、多くの仲間とともに、地道に、石巻の地域のために頑張ってまいります。

第 3 章

福島県

福島県の被害状況

(出典:2016年1月8日発表、警察庁)

〈人的被害〉

死　者	1,613人
行方不明	198人
負傷者	183人

〈建物被害〉

全　壊	1万5,149戸
半　壊	7万8,654戸

〈避難者数(最大時)〉

2012年5月集計　16万4,865人
(出典:福島県発表)

| 山形県 | 宮城県 | 太平洋 |

福島市

相馬市

飯舘村

南相馬市

浪江町

双葉町

大熊町

富岡町

楢葉町

広野町

郡山市

いわき市

福島第一原子力発電所

福島第二原子力発電所

栃木県

茨城県

避難指示の境界線近くで暮らし続ける。

松本さんの自宅は
福島第一原発から
半径約二十一キロに位置する。
故郷を離れる人も多いなか、
松本さん一家は
地域に根を張り、
幸せと復興のために
歩みを続けている。

松本吉弘さん
松本優子さん

（福島県南相馬市）

自宅での生活を選択

優子 地震が起こったとき、私は外出中でした。夫は職場に、長男・拓也と次女・真紀は学校におり、長女の優美は自宅で祖父と過ごしていました。あまりに揺れが大きかったので、「自宅がつぶれてしまったのではないか……」と思ったほどです。

主人に何度も電話しましたが、全然つながりません。気持ちは焦りましたが、「落ち着け、落ち着け」って自分に言い聞かせながら、小学校に次女を迎えに行きました。

吉弘 私はすぐに自宅に向かいました。家につくと、長女たちが家の外で待っていました。家の中にいるのが怖かったのでしょう。

優子 次女を乗せて家に帰ると、私の顔を見た途端、長女がワーッと泣くんです。

吉弘 津波で流されたんじゃないかと心配していたんですよ。その後、高校生の息子も帰ってきて、無事に家族全員が揃いました。

優子 夜十一時ごろだったでしょうか。防災無線で「避難所で生活用品や食料などが不足している」との連絡が入りました。「こんなときに出し惜しみしてはいけない」と思って、私たちは自宅にあった布団やおにぎりなどを持って市役所に行きました。

大勢の若い人も必死になって物資を持ち寄っていました。その姿を見て、「今の日本も捨てたものじゃない」と思ったことを覚えています。

地震発生時、松本さん一家は別々の場所にいたが、全員無事だった。しかし、安心したのもつかの間、福島第一原発の事故により、目に見えない放射能の恐怖に苦しむ生活がはじまった。

優子 原発事故が起きた直後は行政も混乱しており、「屋内退避」の指示が出ては、その指示が解除されるということが続きました。そして、震災翌日の十二日、福島第一原発から半径二十キロ圏内に「避難指示」が出されたんです。

吉弘 その指示が出たときは、自宅が半径二十キロ圏内にあるのかどうかがわからなかったので、家に残りました。あとでわかったことですが、わが家は約二十一キロのところに位置していました。

優子 避難した人たちから「道路が渋滞で、駐車場から出ることさえできない」とか「トイレに行列ができていて、入ることができない」といったメールが次々に届いたので、急いで避難するのを避けたんです。

その後、十四日夕方のニュースで、二号機の格納容器の圧力が高まっていると報じられました。しかし、市民には何の連絡もありません。

そんななか、「中通り（福島県中部）に向かって避難していますが、残っている住人はほとんどいません」とか「私たちもこれから避難します。これま

お世話になりました」というメールが届くんです。「私たちは、このままここにいて大丈夫なのか」と心配になりました。

吉弘 結局、十五日の朝六時ごろに南相馬を離れましたが、その直後に二号機で爆発音がしたと報道されたんです。危機一髪だったと思います。

優子 八十八歳の義父と三人の子どもたちを連れた、行くあてもない避難です。開いている店もないと思い、残っていた食料や調味料、水などを車に詰め込みました。

寝ていた子どもたちを起こし、濡れたハンカチを口に当ててマスクをさせ、防災頭巾を被らせて、ひたすら北に向かいました。

吉弘 なんとか相馬市の知人宅に避難できました。

私たちが避難した日に半径二十〜三十キロ圏内が「屋内退避区域」になったのです。

優子 その知人宅には、十一日間お世話になりました。そして、三月二十六日

84

に一度、南相馬市の自宅に戻ったのですが、子どもたちが「絶対にここにいたい！」って言うんです。見知らぬ土地で不安な日々を過ごすことは、とてもつらかったんだと思います。

吉弘　そこで私たちは腹を決めて、南相馬市の自宅で屋内退避生活を送る道を選びました。

極限の状況で感じた人間の強さ

優子　南相馬市にとどまった人もいれば、避難した人もいます。どちらも本当に苦渋(くじゅう)の決断でした。

吉弘　当初は、屋内退避の地域になかなか支援物資が届かず、パンや缶詰が配給されるのに、二時間待ちの行列ができていました。

優子　子どもたちが通う学校からは最初、「三月は休校」との連絡があり、後

日「四月も……」との連絡がありました。そして突然、「どこかに避難して転校の手続きを取ってください」との知らせがきたのです。驚きました。

吉弘 小学校の体育館は自衛隊の駐屯所になり、高校の体育館は遺体安置所になっていたそうです。結局、半径三十キロ圏外にある学校の校舎が借りられることになり、みんなで毎朝、バスで通学することになりました。

優子 一つの校舎を数校で分けて使いました。一階は「○○小学校」、二階は「××小学校」というように。給食センターは避難所の炊き出しをしていたので、給食はラップに包まれたおにぎり二個とチーズかまぼこ一本、そして牛乳だけだったりしたそうです。

そんな状況ですので、転校する子も出てきました。友達が転校すると、うちの子どもも落ち込んで帰ってきました。親としてはつらかったですね。

吉弘 その後、卒業式は自分たちの元の学校で行おうという話になり、学校の避難は翌年二月末で終わりました。

松本さん一家。右から吉弘さん、長男・拓也さん、次女・真紀さん、長女・優美さん、優子さん

優子 当時の生活をふり返ると、放射能を心配して、室内に外気を一切入れない生活をすることが本当に大変でした。お風呂や料理するときも換気扇を回しませんでした。エアコンもつけず、洗濯も室内干しでした。

屋内退避は人々を分断し、孤立させます。そんな状態で見えない放射能のことを考えると、死の恐怖を感じるのです。だからこそ、近隣の友人が集まったときに感じた嬉しさは忘れられません。

南相馬市は現在、「帰還困難区域」「居住制限区域」「避難指示解除準備区域」「それ以外の地域」に分かれている。南相馬に住み続けている人も引っ越した人も、それぞれの思いを抱えて暮らしている。

吉弘 先日、南相馬の復興を決意し合う集まりが開催され、以前この地域に住んでいた仲間もたくさん駆けつけてくれました。昔からの仲間に会い、みんなとても嬉しそうでしたね。

私は、みんなの表情や様子を見ていて思ったんです。「この地域に残る人、別の地域で新たな生活をはじめる人、みんなそれぞれに使命があるんだな」って。場所は違っていても、心がつながっていることが大切なんですね。

優子 震災から数年経ちましたが、日に日に「こういうつらい経験をするのは私たちで最後にしてほしい」との思いが強くなります。また、それと同時に、この経験を通して「人間はどんなに極限の状態でも強くて優しいんだな」と感

じることができました。

吉弘 本当にそうですね。自然の威力の凄まじさを目の当たりにしましたが、人間の力も凄いと思いました。
　私の家は第一原発から約二十一キロで、避難指示が出た二十キロ圏内の境界線近くに住んでいるわけです。いわば"最前線"ですが、この場所で暮らすことに意味があると思っています。まだまだ、いろんなことが手探りの状態ですが、歩みを止めなければ必ず前に進んでいける、そう確信しています。

原発事故に負けず、避難先で店を再開。郷里の人に元気を贈る。

赤石澤さん夫妻は長年、福島県飯舘村（いいたて）で中華料理店を営んできた。福島第一原発の事故によって避難を余儀なくされたが、「負げでたまっか！」の心で店を再開。郷里の人たちの「憩い（いこ）の場」となっている。

赤石澤　榮（あかいしざわ　さかえ）さん
赤石澤敏子（あかいしざわとしこ）さん

（福島県飯舘村）

食料を持ち寄って避難民を受け入れ

赤石澤さん夫妻が中華料理店「中華琥珀(こはく)」を開業したのは一九七七(昭和五十二)年八月。以来三十年以上にわたり、飯舘村の人たちに愛され続けてきた。
しかし、東日本大震災によって夫妻の人生は一変する。

敏子 あの日は、いつものように夫と一緒に店にいました。地震の瞬間、もの凄(すご)い揺れで私は立っていることもできず、思わずお客さんの足にしがみついていました(笑)。
夫は子どもたちを助けようと、すぐに店を飛び出していきました。店の前はスクールバスの乗降場になっており、地震が起きたときは、下校途中の小学生たちがたくさん店の前にいたんです。

榮 道路が波打つような大きな揺れでした。店の前にいる子どもたちのことが

頭に浮かび、妻や店内のお客さんのことも忘れて（笑）、飛び出しました。急いで子どもたちに「集まれー！」って叫んで、近くの広場へと誘導しました。小さなお子さんを連れた妊婦さんもいましたね。

敏子　その後は停電になったので、とりあえず店に残っていたご飯でおにぎりを作ってご近所に配ったり、漬物なんかも、みんな配りましたね。

榮　そんなことで、俺のところで炊き出しをしてるって噂が広まって、「違うんだ。これはご近所に配るんだ」って説明したりしてね（笑）。電気は止まっているけど、うちは電気じゃなくて業務用のガス釜だったんで、ご飯が炊けたんです。ですから、「お米持ってきたら炊くよ」って。

幸い店は無事でした。じつは震災の少し前に店舗改装をやって、柱の補強をしていたんです。だから、そのときは「店内を片付ければ営業を再開できる。守られた」って思いましたね。

しかし、その後の福島第一原発の事故によって、赤石澤さんの暮らしも激変を余儀なくされた。飯舘村はほぼ全域が第一原発から三十キロ圏外にあるため、当初は避難区域にならず、他地域からの避難住民を受け入れた。

榮　公民館のテレビで村長たちと原発事故のニュースを見ながら、「やっぱりか」なんて話していたけど、こんなに大事になるなんて誰も思ってなかった。そんなときに電話がかかってきて、これから何千人と避難してくるって。そこからは〝戦争〟だよ。

敏子　飯舘村ははじめ、避難区域ではありませんでした。逆に南相馬市などの沿岸部から、たくさんの避難者を受け入れていたんです。

榮　渋滞で車も並んじゃって、全然動かない。俺たちは交代しながら二十四時間態勢で受け入れですよ。四千人ほどの方が飯舘村に避難してこられた。私は消防団の副分団長をしていたので、避難者の受け入れ準備や誘導に走り回りま

93　赤石澤 榮・敏子

した。

避難所になった公民館や体育館に、村の人たちが自分の家にあるストーブや毛布などを持ち寄りました。女性の皆さんには三交代で炊き出しをやっていただいて、朝昼晩と四千個のおにぎりを配って歩いたんです。備蓄してあった食料も全部持ち寄りました。

敏子　一番困ったのはガソリン。村には全然入ってこない。村の住民は一人一〇リットルという給油カードをもらっていたけれど、村外から避難してきた人に分けられるガソリンはないわけです。

ここ（飯舘村）からさらに避難したくても、ガソリンがない。なんとかしてくれって頼まれても、どうしようもない。

榮　でも、子どもさんを連れた人なんかが泣きながら来るわけよ。だから、俺たちの券をあげたりしましたね。

避難先で店を再開

震災から一カ月が経った四月十一日。第一原発から二十キロ圏外にある飯舘村など五市町村にも避難指示が出された。

敏子 飯舘村は福島第一原発から四十キロほども離れていたので、避難指示が出されても実感が湧(わ)きませんでした。「村の景色は何も変わらないのに、なんで出ていかなければいけないのか」という思いでした。

榮 そのときも、俺ら消防団のメンバーは自分たちを後回しにして、まずは避難してきていた人を優先的に避難させました。次に住人を避難させて、みんなが避難したのを確認してから、最後に避難しました。自分のことよりも、とにかく村のこと、避難者のことしか頭にありませんでしたね。

でも、村を離れたくないという人が三人ほどいましたから、何度も行って話

しましたよ。大変だというより、あれをしなきゃいけない、これをしなきゃいけないって、目の前のことをやるだけでした。

その後、赤石澤さん夫妻は福島県飯坂町(いいざか)にある県の借り上げ住宅に、母と三人で入居した。

榮　避難後、一回だけ村に戻ったことがありました。人が住んでないというのは、これだけ淋(さび)しいんだって実感しましたね。しかも、山奥だから、電気もない、何にもない。シーンとして、凄(すさ)まじい世界だね。そういう世界を見ると、今の幸せが一瞬でストーンと崩れて、暗闇が押し寄せるんだなって。光のない世界が。

店にも立ち寄ってみたんですが、店内にはフライパンや鍋(なべ)が散乱していまし

96

た。でも、きちんと収納していた食器類は、ほとんどが割れずに残っていたんです。それを見たとき、「もう一度やってやる！　負けてたまっか！」という思いが込み上げてきました。

それから、一からやり直すつもりで、とにかく店を再開しようと、避難先で物件を探しはじめました。

敏子　でも、いい物件だと思っても家賃が高かったりして、なかなか希望に沿う物件が見つかりませんでした。なかば諦(あきら)めかけていたときに、飯舘村から「福島市の仮設住宅で店を出さないか」という話が舞い込んできたんです。建物はプレハブですが、建築費用はかからず、開店経費の四分の三も補助が出るという好条件でした。それまで物件がなかなか見つからなかったことも、全部意味があったんだと思いました。

「中華琥珀」を再オープンできたのは、二〇一一年十一月でしたね。

榮　この仮設住宅には五百人ほどの人が入居しているんですが、全員が飯舘村

97　赤石澤　榮・敏子

仮設住宅に再オープンした「中華琥珀」

からの避難民なんです。もともとの常連さんも多くいましたから、当初は常連さんや近所の人たちが来てくれればいいと思っていたんです。ところが、オープン初日には、なんと三百人ものお客さんが来てくれた。店の外に行列ができるほどでした。皆さん本当に店の再開を喜んでくれて、「看板を見ただけで涙が出てきた」と言ってくれる人もいました。

敏子 この店が皆さんの「憩いの場」になってくれたら、と思っています。狭い仮設住宅での生活は本当に大変で

すし、一人暮らしの方も多くいます。そのような方々に、「ここに来たら、冗談を言ったり、笑い合ったりできる」と感じてもらえる場所でありたいと願っています。

榮　ありがたいことに、多くの方が「ここでずっと店を続けてくれ」って言ってくれるんです。そういう方がいるかぎり、店を続けようと思っています。
　それと同時に、飯舘村が避難解除になって帰村がはじまれば、飯舘村でも「中華琥珀」を再開しようと思っています。
　放射能の心配もありますし、帰村しない人も多いと思います。それでも、私は飯舘村で店を再開したい。それは地域への恩返しですよね。
　これからも「負げでたまっか！」の気持ちで、飯舘村の復興のために頑張っていきたいと思います。

99　赤石澤 榮・敏子

震災後の奮闘を支えた笑顔のふれあいと仲間の絆。

金澤さん夫妻が暮らす広野(ひろの)町は、福島第一原発から三十キロ圏内にある。
原発事故のあと、夫妻は自身も避難を余儀なくされながら、一貫して被災者を支え、励ましを送り続けてきた。

金澤金治(かなざわかねじ)さん
金澤清子(かなざわきよこ)さん

（福島県広野町）

とっさの判断で高台へ避難

清子 地震が起きたとき、私はいわき市にある知人宅にいました。地震は、今までに経験したことのないもの凄い揺れで、慌てて外に出ましたが、つかまるものもなかったので、みんなで肩を組みながら、揺れが収まるのを待ちました。市内に出て見ると、マンホールのふたは吹き飛び、道路はあちこちが壊れてガタガタになっていました。その後、「津波がくる」という情報を聞いたので、慌てて山側の道路を通り、車で広野町にある自宅へ向かいました。途中、ずぶ濡れで道路に立っていた女性を乗せてあげました。津波に車を流され、命からがら逃げてきたそうです。本当に信じられないことの連続でした。

金治 私は、広野町にある火力発電所で建築関係の業務に従事していました。そこは福島第一原発から約二十キロ離れたところにあり、地震が起きたとき、私は五号西建屋の一階でオイル交換作業をしていました。

避難しようと思い、一旦、他社の作業員たちとともに、建屋地下に待機しました。しかし、「もし津波がきたら、建屋に水が入り、出られなくなる」と判断した私は、作業員とともに施設内の高台に避難しました。
高台に到着して間もなく潮が引きはじめ、発電所近くにある釣り場の海底が丸見えになっていました。やがて巨大な鉄板のような真っ黒い津波が襲ってきたんです。まるで映画を見ているようで、現実のこととは思えませんでした。
津波は計七回襲ってきました。そのうちの二回目がとくに大きく、発電所のあらゆるものを押し流していきました。
私の車も流されたので、その日は仕方なく、四キロほど離れた自宅まで歩いて帰りました。

翌十二日には福島第一原発の一号機で水素爆発が起こった。金澤さんが暮らす広野町は第一原発から二十〜三十キロ離れた地域にあるが、十三日には全町

民に避難指示が出された。

清子 十二日の夕方ごろに、町のスピーカーから「避難してください」という自主避難を促(うなが)すアナウンスが流れてきました。でも、なぜ避難しなければならないのか、どこに避難すればいいのか、まったく知らされませんでした。

金治 私はすぐに風向きを見ました。すると、南から北に向かって風が吹いていたので、風上である南へ向かって逃げました。

清子 とりあえず、実家のあるいわき市に向かいました。ところが、避難の途中、創価学会の仲間から携帯に電話があり、「いわき文化会館」に大勢の人が避難してきていることがわかったのです。私はその地域の学会の責任者をしていましたので、実家ではなく、すぐにいわき文化会館に直行しました。

金治 私たちが到着したころには、三十〜四十名ほどの方が避難していました。

清子 その後すぐ、いわき文化会館に近い地域に避難指示が出されたので、そ

103　金澤金治・清子

の日のうちに、より原発から遠い「いわき平和会館」へ移動しました。

金治 道路は大混乱していたし、道もでこぼこで、どうやって走ったか覚えていませんが、なんとかみんなで平和会館に到着しました。

清子 その日はもの凄く寒かったのですが、いわき平和会館は電気が通じていて、暖房も入ったので助かりました。

笑顔でみんなを元気に

清子 まずなにより、食料の確保が最優先でした。近所の学会の仲間にお願いして、お米や野菜を提供してもらったり、炊飯器(すいはんき)を貸してもらったりして、なんとかやりくりしました。

最初はおじやを作りましたが、紙コップ半分ずつくらいしかお配りできませんでした。その後、二〜三日経ってから、全国のメンバーから救援物資が届く

104

ようになりました。本当にありがたかったです。

金治 平和会館には百三十名くらいの避難者がおり、学会員以外の方もいらっしゃいました。避難翌日からは、みんなで協力して生活するために、掃除班、炊事班、水汲み班などの役割体制を組みました。ありがたいことに、料理が得意な人や消臭方法に詳しいトイレ診断士、看護師さんなど、それぞれの分野で秀でた方がいたんです。

清子 会館の雰囲気づくりには気を配りました。皆さん、今後のことが不安ですので、どうしても雰囲気が暗くなってしまうんです。ですから少しでも「元気になってもらいたい」と思い、私自身、笑顔でいることを心がけましたし、みんなを笑わせることに力を注ぎました。

金治 朝食のときは、「パンパカパーン、パンパンパン、パンパカパーン、本日の朝のメニューを紹介します！ 超一流の秋田米で作ったライスボールと完熟バナナです！」「飲み物はサントリーのビール！」と言いたいところですが、

いわき平和会館での救援物資搬入の様子（2011年3月15日）
©Seikyo Shimbun

サントリーの水でした！」なんてやるわけです。これにはそのつど笑いが起きて、雰囲気が一気に軽くなりましたね。

清子 今だから言えますが、心の中には、「とても笑顔になんてなれない」という思いもありました。それでも、笑顔でいることが皆さんに希望を与えると思って、人と接していましたね。

金治 学会の会館は正式な避難場所ではなかったので、十日間で閉館しました。閉館を前に、避難者お一人お一人と面談して、どこに避難するのかうか

106

がいました。そして、避難先までの距離を想定して、それぞれに必要なガソリンを手配していただき、皆さんを送り出しました。

平和会館をあとにした金澤さんは一時、神奈川県の娘さんのところに身を寄せたが、すぐにいわき市内にアパートを借り、避難指示解除後、広野町に戻った。しかし、避難した人の半数近くが、今も広野町に戻ってきていないという。

金治　会社から仕事再開の連絡があり、四月下旬に私一人で自宅に戻りました。住んでいる人もほとんどいないし、なぜか鳥の声が全然聞こえない。腹をすかせた犬がくっついてくるばかりで、ともかく不気味でしたね。仕事場は見るも無残で、毎日、掃除や片付けに明け暮れました。それでも、四カ月で復旧させたときは、みんなで万歳（ばんざい）しました。

清子　私たち夫婦はわが家に戻ったけど、帰りたくても帰れない人も大勢いま

す。そうした全国各地に避難した仲間とは、今も連絡を取り合っています。

金治　原発事故等による避難者の集い「うつくしまフェニックスグループ」として、定期的に会い、励まし合っています。第一回は、震災から三カ月が経った六月に開催されたのですが、久しぶりにみんなと会ったときは、涙、涙で言葉が出ませんでした。

清子　本当に。顔を見ただけで、心がほっとしましたし、元気が出ました。みんなで手を取り合って、再会を喜び合いました。

その後、東京や福島などでも開催してきましたが、「震災後は涙腺が緩んで困るね」なんて、話をしています（笑）。

金治　苦難を一緒に乗り越えた仲間だから、とくに強い絆で結ばれていると思います。これからも、励まし合いながら、ともに前に進んでいきたいと思っています。

108

第4章

救援活動を
ふり返る

東日本大震災と「励ましの絆」。

――震災発生後、
創価学会の会館は
多数の避難者を受け入れた。
青年部員をはじめ
多くの人々が、
不眠不休で
災害対策に取り組んだ。

創価学会東北総合青年部長
山根幹雄
（やまね みきお）

震災直後からはじまった避難者支援

「もしかしたら、このまま建物が倒壊して死んでしまうかもしれない」
地震発生直後、これまでに経験したことのない激しい揺れのなかで感じた私の実感です。

東日本大震災が発生した二〇一一年三月十一日、私は勤務する仙台市内の創価学会東北文化会館にいました。三分間余りの揺れは本当に長く感じられました。

揺れが収まった瞬間、一斉に機械類の警告ランプが点滅し、ブザーが鳴り響きました。私は「災害対策本部を立ち上げます！」と叫び、ただちに東京の学会本部と電話交信しました。そして、ボイラーをはじめとする館内の機械などを点検し、在館者にケガ人がいないかを確認しました。

当時、私は宮城県創価学会の青年部のリーダーの一人でしたので、同僚の皆

山根幹雄

さんとともに、県内各会館の状況掌握にも全力を尽くしました。しかし、各地の会館とはなかなか連絡が取れませんでした。のちにわかったことですが、県内では、気仙沼と石巻の会館が津波に襲われていました。

地震発生から約二十分後には、東北文化会館に最初の避難者が訪れました。やがて近隣の方々が次々に避難してこられ、午後十一時ごろには館内の避難者の数は三百人にも達していました。

最終的に今回の震災では、東北文化会館に一千人、宮城県内十四会館では三千人の方々を受け入れ、学会全体としては四十二会館で最大五千人の被災者を受け入れました。

東北文化会館が避難所として運営されたのは約一カ月半でした。運営にあたった私たちの思いは「避難されてきた方の安全と健康だけは、絶対に守りたい」との一点でした。

しかし、電気・ガス・水道というライフラインが止まり、大震災の混乱に

112

資料① 創価学会会館での避難者の救援・保護

東北の被災3県および茨城県、千葉県の計42の会館で、地域の住民を中心に約5,000人を一時避難所として受け入れた。主な会館の最大収容時人数は以下の通り。

※避難者のうち会員と非会員の割合は会館によりかなり異なるが、宮城県の若林平和会館、古川文化会館など、大半が非会員で占められたところも多い。

宮城県／避難会館総数：14会館	
東北文化会館（仙台市）	約1,000人
若林平和会館（仙台市）	約600人
古川文化会館（大崎市）	約800人
石巻文化会館（石巻市）	約150人
石巻平和会館（石巻市）	約70人

岩手県／避難会館総数：6会館	
岩手文化会館（盛岡市）	約40人
釜石文化会館（釜石市）	約40人
一関文化会館（一関市）	約20人

福島県／避難会館総数：9会館	
福島文化会館（郡山市）	約200人
福島平和会館（福島市）	約150人
いわき平和会館（いわき市）	約150人
相馬会館（相馬市）	約80人
原町文化会館（南相馬市）	約50人

茨城県／避難会館総数：3会館	
勝田文化会館（ひたちなか市）	約20人

千葉県／避難会館総数：10会館	
船橋池田講堂（船橋市）	約230人
旭文化会館（旭市）	約35人

山根幹雄

よって行政からの支援物資も望めません。どうしたら避難者の皆さんの安心と安全を確保できるのか、非常に悩み、心を尽くしました。

第一の問題は食料です。三百人もの避難者の食事をどうするかに思い至ったのは、震災当日の午後十一時すぎになってからでした。明日の食料のめどが立っていなかったのです。

職員用食堂には無洗米(むせんまい)がありました。そこで、近隣の会員の方から家庭用炊飯器(はんき)を八台提供していただき、おにぎりを作ることにしました。しかし、一台の炊飯器で一回に炊けるご飯の分量はかぎられており、おにぎりにすると十五個程度しか作れません。身を寄せてこられる被災者の数は刻一刻と増える一方です。

非常用電源で炊飯器をフル稼働(かどう)し、会館の管理者や職員、地元の会員が徹夜で作業にあたりました。その結果、翌朝までになんとか千個の小さなおにぎりが完成し、間に合わせることができたのです。

114

震災当日、山形県米沢市では青年部が救援物資を積み込み、被災地に向かった
©Seikyo Shimbun

　他県の学会組織も迅速に動いてくださいました。震災発生から十二時間後の十二日午前二時すぎには、山形から緊急支援物資の第一便が届きました。寸断された交通網を縫うようにして届けてくださったのです。おかげで早朝には、おにぎりの他に、水やソーセージなども用意することができました。

　新潟から五千五百個ものおにぎりが届いたのは、震災翌日のことでした。二〇〇四年に中越地震、〇七年に中越沖地震を経験している新潟のメンバーは、こちらからの要請を待たずに、重

油や飲料水、パン、簡易トイレなどの救援物資をピストン輸送で何度も届けてくださいました。

大きさや形が違う手作りのおにぎりと、そこに添えられていた「負けないで」「頑張って」「私たちも祈っています。共に、乗り越えていきましょう」との言葉には、全員が目頭を熱くし、感謝の思いで食べました。

全国各地から送られてくる支援物資や手紙、そこに込められた真心が、精神的にも肉体的にもギリギリのところで踏ん張っていた私たちを支えてくれました。

食料とともに大変だったのはトイレの問題です。館内に災害用の簡易トイレを備蓄（びちく）していましたが、使い方を知っている避難者はほとんどいません。そのため職員が懐中電灯を持ち、真っ暗な会館の中で防寒着を着て交代で洗面所の入り口に常駐（じょうちゅう）。二十四時間態勢で使用法の説明にあたりました。トイレには臭（にお）いが充満するなか、「避難された方々の役に立つなら」と、この大変な役割を

116

資料② 創価学会の支援ネットワーク

震災発生直後より、必要物資を集め、全国各方面から支援の手が差し伸べられた。途中の道路が寸断されていたため、フェリーで海を渡って岩手に駆けつけた北海道の組織をはじめ、青森、秋田、山形、新潟、関西、東京などで、被災地である東北への救援態勢が敷かれた。

〈主な救援物資〉

創価学会として合計約64万1,700点を独自のネットワークを通じて提供。内訳は以下の通り。

簡易トイレ	約6万点
衣類(防寒着、シャツ、ズボン、肌着等)	約2万4,000点
寝具(毛布、布団等)	約4,700点
生活用品(介護用品[おむつ・尿取りパット等])	約18万3,000点
飲料・食料品(おにぎり、ゼリー、果物、保存食、飲料、菓子、調味料等)	約29万6,000点
薬品類(風邪薬、胃腸薬、うがい薬、包帯等)	約4万600点
備品類(燃料[重油・軽油・ガソリン：約8,320リットル、発電機等]、備品[血圧計、自転車、ホワイトボード、洗濯機・乾燥機、ポット、カセットコンロ、カセットガスボンベ等])	約3万3,400点

率先して担ってくれたメンバーの姿勢には、頭が下がりました。館内の衛生環境にも気を使いました。寒い時期でしたので風邪やインフルエンザなどを蔓延させてはならないと、アルコール消毒やマスクの着用などを徹底しました。

避難所生活三日目からは、一日のスケジュールを張り出し、「食事」「ラジオ体操」「換気」「清掃」などのリズムをつくりました。

避難された方には、津波被害に遭った方もいれば、家族の安否がわからない状況の方もいました。皆が不安な気持ちを抱えています。だからこそ、「おはようございます！」「お体は大丈夫ですか？」と、元気な声かけを心がけました。

朝には、カーテンを開けて、ラジオ体操。声を出してもらうことで、ふさぎ込んだ気持ちが少しでも晴れてほしいとの一心でした。医師や看護師のメンバーに協力を要請し、健康相談も開始しました。

資料③ 創価学会・SGIからの義援金

2011年3月30、31日に、学会本部として義援金を以下の自治体に寄託した。

宮城県	1億円
岩手県	1億5千万円
福島県	1億5千万円
千葉県	1千万円
茨城県	3千万円
仙台市	1億円
総　額	5億4千万円

※会員個人からの義援金ならびに物資の受け入れについては、より効果的な支援のために、日本赤十字社などの専門機関を通じて行うよう、「聖教新聞」を通じて促した。そのため、創価学会として直接の義援金の受け入れは行っていない。

創価学会インタナショナル（SGI）の各国（16カ国・地域）組織からも、以下の義援金が関係団体等へ寄託された。

台湾	126,400 USドル	アメリカ	50,000 USドル
香港	266,528 USドル	シンガポール	573,669 USドル
カナダ	10,383 USドル	フィリピン	60,797 USドル
マレーシア	348,374 USドル	インド	478,808 USドル
タイ	49,538 USドル	スイス	10,000 USドル
ブラジル	61,690 USドル	ペルー	8,000 USドル
インドネシア	20,475 USドル	パラグアイ	7,843 USドル
韓国	153,621 USドル	総　額	2,238,617 USドル（約2.5億円*）
マカオ	12,491 USドル		

＊2016年2月12日のレート換算

山根幹雄

"一人に会える喜び"

私が勤務する東北文化会館は、県内の会館の管理、および組織活動の支援をしています。

四日目になっても、気仙沼会館の状況がまったくつかめていなかったので、私が向かうことになりました。

道路の崩壊などにより、普段の二倍以上の五時間をかけて、気仙沼に到着しました。線路をつたってなんとか気仙沼会館に行こうとするものの、瓦礫に阻まれてしまい、たどりつけませんでした。

そこで一旦、気仙沼に一番近い、とはいっても車で一時間半かかる登米市の会館に、気仙沼の対策本部をつくることになりました。それから約一カ月間は、そこに寝泊まりして、気仙沼の皆さんの支援をしました。

震災後、日増しに想像を絶する甚大な被害状況が明らかになるにつれて、私

創価学会の東北文化会館に避難した人たちに朝食が配布された
（2011年3月12日）
©Seikyo Shimbun

　自身、何度も無力感に襲われました。
　なぜ東北でなければならなかったのか。そこに住む人々が、また大切な仲間が、なぜこれほどの苦しみに遭わなければならないのか。大切な家族を亡くさなければならないのか──。
　不条理といえばあまりに不条理な現実に、言いようのない悲しみで胸が張り裂けそうになり、何度も涙し、心が折れそうになったときもありました。
　そうした絶望感がピークに達していた三月十六日の「聖教新聞」に、池田名誉会長からのメッセージが掲載され

ました。

　地震が収まった瞬間から全力で救援活動に奔走していた私たちの心は、あらがいがたい自然の猛威へのあきらめや無力感、これから一体どうなっていくのだろうという先が見えない不安感で覆い尽くされそうになっていました。それだけに「いかなる苦難も『心の財』だけは絶対に壊せない」「逝去なされたご親族やご友人の追善回向を懇ろに行わせていただいております。本当に残念でなりませんが、生命は永遠であり、生死を超えて結ばれています」「断じて負けるな！　勇気を持て！　希望を持て！」とのメッセージは、多くの会員が前を見つめて力強く歩き出すためのきっかけとなり、心の支えとなりました。

　気仙沼の支援にあたっては、会員かどうかを問わず、自宅に避難されている方などにも支援物資を配布させていただきました。日頃から地域社会に根差している方は、周辺で孤立している人のことまで掌握されているため、多くの方

122

清掃ボランティア「かたし隊」の活動風景（2011年6月5日、石巻市内）
©Seikyo Shimbun

に物資をお届けできました。

また、瓦礫の片付けなど個別の要望が出るようになってきたので、そうした対応もしました。これについては、地域の青年部員が自主的に名乗り出てくれました。こうしたボランティアチームは被災地の各地で結成され、のちに、「片付ける」という意味と「勝たせる」という両方の意味が込められた、「かたし隊」との名前が付きました。必死で取り組んでくださった皆さんへの感謝は尽きません。

また、会員の皆さんの状況の把握も

進めました。とはいっても、元の家から避難されている方が多いのはもちろん、電話も通じません。津波等でもともとの名簿が手に入らない地域も多かったため、人づてで情報を得て、一人一人の避難先、被災状況を確認し、一覧化していきました。

一人一人のお宅にうかがうなかで、以前からの知人に出会えると、「元気でいてくださった」「本当によかった」と〝一人に会える喜び〟を感じました。そのときは〝人に会う〟という当たり前のことが新鮮な感動でした。また気仙沼会館の状況も確認しましたが、二階の床上まで浸水しており、あらゆる備品が使い物にならなくなり、建物としての維持も困難になっていました。

しかし、そんな状況のなかでも、不思議なことに、小学生の学会愛唱歌の手書きの模造紙だけが、無傷で残っていました。未来を象徴する出来事に、会員の皆さんは本当に喜んでいました。

資料④ 創価学会の人的支援

①会館運営ボランティア

一時避難所運営 （岩手県、宮城県、福島県、茨城県、千葉県）	約12,500人
帰宅困難者受け入れ（東京都）	約100人
合　　計	約12,600人

②物資救援ボランティア

北海道（物資調達、輸送など）	約700人
山形県（物資調達、輸送など）	約400人
岩手県（内陸部からの物資調達、輸送など）	約240人
福島県（内陸部からの物資調達、輸送など）	約420人
青森県（炊き出し、物資輸送など）	約110人
新潟県（物資調達、輸送など）	約2,200人
首都圏（物資調達、輸送など）	約140人
合　　計	約4,210人

※数字は出動したボランティアの延べ人数。
※この数字には宗教法人創価学会として行った復興支援業務に携わった職員数、および海外の会員によるボランティア数は含まれていない。

被災地域の会員たちは、地域のコミュニティとの深いつながりを生かし救援活動にあたった。具体的には、会員および地域住民の安否確認と励まし、一般避難所への救援物資の供給、行政・民間企業との協力、在日外国人の支援、不足物資についての情報伝達などに取り組んだ。医師や看護師のメンバーによる健康相談、弁護士・公認会計士・税理士などのメンバーによる法律相談、美容師のグループによるボランティアカットなども行われた。
その後の復興期も支援活動が継続された。

山根幹雄

災害に負けない社会づくり

　震災から間もなく五年が経とうとしています。被災地の現状は細分化する一方です。津波の跡（あと）さえ見えなくなっている街もあれば、町全体が被災したために、道路から新しくデザインするように工事が進む地域もあります。復興住宅で新しい生活をはじめた人もいれば、仮設住宅に住み続けている人や、まだ故郷に戻れない人さえいます。

　それでも、一人一人の心の声に耳を傾け、どこまでも苦しみや悲しみに寄り添い続けるなかで、少しでもその人が勇気と希望を持って人生を前向きに生きていけるように、励まし続けるしかないのではないかと思っています。

　そうした一対一の励ましの後押しになればということで、二〇一四年からは、創価学会音楽隊が「希望の絆（きずな）」コンサートを開催しています。各部門の全国大会で金賞を受賞している創価グロリア吹奏楽団、関西吹奏楽団、創価ルネサン

スバンガード、しなの合唱団の四つの楽団が、被災地域の文化施設や仮設住宅の集会所などで行うコンサートで、累計で七十回を超えました。
 音楽隊の皆さんは首都圏や関西圏で暮らしている青年であり、それぞれ仕事や家庭を抱えています。そうしたメンバーが、どうしたら被災者の皆さんに励ましを送れるかと悩み抜いたうえで奏でる演奏、また、聴衆に「聞かせる」のではなく、工夫をこらして聴衆と「一緒に作り上げていく」演奏には、言葉に表すことのできない感動が広がっています。
 なかでも印象に残っているのは、被災者の方々と音楽隊員との直接の交流の場面です。音楽隊のメンバーが皆さんを見送る際に、被災者の方が涙ながらに、「絶対に負けないよ。みんなの思いに応えるからね」と力強く語られておりました。真心に真心で応えてくれたことに、「私のほうが励まされる思いでした」
と、音楽隊員は語っていました。
 救援し励ます側と救援され励まされる側といった、固定的な関係ではなく、

山根幹雄

相互が励ましを送りそれがつながっていく光景に、人間の強さを見た思いでした。

震災はあまりに多くのものを奪ってしまいましたが、もし得られたものがあるとするなら、こうした「励ましの絆」の重要性だと思います。その励ましは、文字通り日本中、世界中から寄せられました。

私たちはこの震災の出来事を、なんとしても次世代に継承して、さらに災害に負けない社会づくりに尽力してまいる決意です。

<Human Support>

1) Operational support volunteers at Soka Gakkai centers that served as shelter

For operation of temporary shelter (Iwate, Miyagi, Fukushima, Ibaraki, Chiba prefectures)	approx. 12,500 people
Shelter for people who could not return home on March 11 (Tokyo)	approx. 100
Total	approx. 12,600

2) Logistic support volunteers

Hokkaido (procurement, transportation, etc.)	approx. 700 people
Yamagata Prefecture (procurement, transportation, etc.)	approx. 400
Iwate Prefecture (procurement and transportation from inland areas, etc.)	approx. 240
Fukushima Prefecture (procurement and transportation from inland areas, etc.)	approx. 420
Aomori Prefecture (cooking, procurement and transportation, etc.)	approx. 110
Niigata (procurement, transportation, etc.)	approx. 2,200
Tokyo metropolitan area (procurement, transportation, etc.)	approx. 140
Total:	approx. 4,210

*The above figures are total headcounts provided.
*The figures do not include Soka Gakkai management and staff who participated in reconstruction operations conducted by the Soka Gakkai itself as a religious institution, nor Soka Gakkai's overseas members who participated in voluntary activities.

Soka Gakkai members of the affected areas participated in relief activities utilizing their strong ties with people of their respective local communities. Specifically, they undertook activities such as supplying emergency goods to various public shelters, cooperating with local administrations and private companies, supporting foreign residents in their areas, transmitting information regarding the goods in short supply, etc.

Soka Gakkai members who were doctors and nurses served as health consultants while lawyers, public accountants, tax accountants and other specialists gave free legal advices, and the group of hairdressers gave free haircuts, etc.

Support activities continuing as recovery progresses.

March 11, 2011: More Than Survival

\<Relief Funds\>

On March 30 and 31, 2011, the following relief funds were donated in the name of the Soka Gakkai to respective local authorities:

To: Miyagi Prefecture:	¥ 100,000,000
Iwate Prefecture:	¥ 150,000,000
Fukushima Prefecture:	¥ 150,000,000
Chiba Prefecture	¥ 10,000,000
Ibaraki Prefecture	¥ 30,000,000
Sendai City	¥ 100,000,000
Total:	¥ 540,000,000

*In order to render monetary support more effectively, Soka Gakkai members were recommended through the organization's newspaper, the Seikyo Shimbun, to make individual donations of relief funds and supplies through the Japan Red Cross or other specialized agencies. Accordingly, the Soka Gakkai did not accept any donations from members.

Relief funds were also deposited to the accounts of involved organizations by 16 overseas organizations of Soka Gakkai International (SGI) as follows:

Taiwan:	US$ 126,400	USA:	US$ 50,000
Hong Kong:	US$ 266,528	Singapore:	US$ 573,669
Canada:	US$ 10,383	Philippines:	US$ 60,797
Malaysia:	US$ 348,374	India:	US$ 478,808
Thailand:	US$ 49,538	Switzerland:	US$ 10,000
Brazil:	US$ 61,690	Peru:	US$ 8,000
Indonesia:	US$ 20,475	Paraguay:	US$ 7,843
Republic of Korea:	US$ 153,621	Total:	US$ 2,238,617
Macao:	US$ 12,491		

(approx. JPY 250,000,000 at the exchange rate as of February 12, 2016)

(2) Support network

Starting immediately after the earthquake, all-out support rushed in from Soka Gakkai members throughout the country. Beginning with the Soka Gakkai's Hokkaido group, where members scraped up necessary goods and brought them by the first available ferry to Iwate, rescue arrangements were set up in Aomori, Akita, Yamagata, Niigata, Kansai, Tokyo and so on, despite the transport difficulty that resulted from damage to the road and rail network.

<Main Relief Supplies>

A total of 641,700 relief items were delivered through the Soka Gakkai's own network (breakdown follows):

Portable toilets	approx. 60,000 pieces
Clothing (cold weather clothing, shirts, trousers, underclothes, etc.)	approx. 24,000
Bedding (blankets, etc.)	approx. 4,700
Living ware (nursing care goods [diapers, incontinence articles, etc.])	approx. 183,000
Beverages, foodstuffs (rice-balls, jelly, fruits, preserved foods, drinks, snacks, condiments, etc.)	approx. 296,000
Medical supplies (medicine for colds, stomach, mouthwash, bandages, etc.)	approx. 46,000
Appliances and equipment (generators, blood pressure gauges, bicycles, washing machines, dryers, water pots, portable gas burners, gas cartridge, etc. with fuel including heavy oil, light oil and gasoline, totaling approx. 8,320 liters)	approx. 33,400

March 11, 2011: More Than Survival

Soka Gakkai Relief Activities Background Information

(1) Relief and protection of refugees

Altogether, forty-two centers in three prefectures (Iwate, Miyagi and Fukushima) of the Tohoku region and two prefectures (Ibaraki and Chiba) of the Kanto region provided temporary shelter to about 5,000 people, mainly local residents of the respective regions. The numbers of people taking refuge at major centers were as follows:

*The proportion of non-members who took refuge at local Soka Gakkai centers varied from center to center. However, at many centers, such as Wakabayashi Peace Center and Furukawa Culture Center in Miyagi Prefecture, most of the refugees were non-members.

Miyagi Prefecture - Number of centers used as shelter: 14	
Tohoku Culture Center (Sendai)	approx. 1000 people
Wakabayashi Peace Center (Sendai)	approx. 600
Furukawa Culture Center (Osaki)	approx. 800
Ishinomaki Culture Center (Ishinomaki)	approx. 150
Ishinomaki Peace Center (Ishinomaki)	approx. 70
Iwate Prefecture - Number of centers used as shelter: 6	
Iwate Culture Center (Morioka)	approx. 40 people
Kamaishi Culture Center (Kamaishi)	approx. 40
Ichinoseki Culture Center (Ichinoseki)	approx. 20
Fukushima Prefecture - Number of centers used as shelter: 9	
Fukushima Culture Center (Koriyama)	approx. 200 people
Fukushima Peace Center (Fukushima)	approx. 150
Iwaki Peace Center (Iwaki)	approx. 150
Soma Center (Soma)	approx. 80
Haramachi Culture Center (Minamisoma)	approx. 50
Ibaraki Prefecture - Number of centers used as shelter: 3	
Katsuta Culture Center (Hitachinaka)	approx. 20 people
Chiba Prefecture - Number of centers used as shelter: 10	
Funabashi Ikeda Auditorium (Funabashi)	approx. 230 people
Asahi Culture Center (Asahi)	approx. 35

it, that would be the "networks of encouragement" that emerged in the wake of the disaster. Such encouragement literally came from all over Japan and the world.

My determination is to help transmit memories of "March 11" on to future generations, and in the process contribute to building a society that is resilient in the face of disaster.

Vanguard, and the Shinano Male Choir (each the winner of first prizes at national competitions), have held more than seventy concerts at cultural facilities and meeting rooms of temporary housing units in the disaster area.

The musicians in these groups are all residents of the Tokyo and Kansai areas, and most have jobs and families of their own to care for. In seeking to encourage audiences who have been the victims of disaster, these groups have not simply held performances, but have worked to involve their audiences in "performances that we build together." Words cannot convey the emotional impact of such efforts.

My most memorable recollection of these events is of the direct interactions that took place between ensemble members and disaster victims. Speaking with determination, the victims said, "We will never give up. We will rise to all your expectations." The musicians, hearing such words, later said, "It felt like we were the ones being encouraged."

What I gained from witnessing such chains of mutual encouragement — a sharp departure from the customary notion that assistance flows from relief workers to victims — was a sense of the strength of the human spirit.

The earthquake and tsunami took away so much, but I realized that if there is anything positive that came out of

But by chance, a sheet of imitation vellum inscribed with a Gakkai song for children had survived unscathed. As this song was a symbol of the future, members were delighted with their discovery.

Building a disaster-resistant society

Now almost five years have passed. Conditions in the disaster area vary greatly. Whereas all traces of the tsunami's aftermath have disappeared from some towns, in other places entire towns were destroyed, and even roads had to be rebuilt according to new plans. While some people have started new lives in reconstructed homes, others continue living in temporary housing, or are unable to return to their home towns at all.

Still, I think there is no alternative to listening to words that come from the heart of each individual still locked in the vise of suffering and sorrow, and to continue encouraging such people to find courage to continue living life positively with hope for the future.

Giving a boost to such one-on-one encouragement, from 2014 the Soka Gakkai Music Corps began holding a "Building Bonds of Hope" series of concerts. Four musical ensembles, the Soka Gloria Wind Orchestra, the Soka Gakkai Kansai Wind Orchestra, the Soka Renaissance

area as well. Here, the region's young people stepped up and provided substantial assistance. These volunteer teams formed throughout the disaster region, and were later dubbed the 'Katashi-tai' (Katashi Corps), a play on the word 'katasu,' which has the dual connotations of 'cleaning up' and 'promoting victory over hardship'. I can't begin to convey the depth of my gratitude to all those who contributed assistance.

We've also made much progress on determining the status of our members. This has been a challenge, as many people had to leave their homes, and therefore cannot be reached by telephone. Membership lists for many areas were lost during the tsunami, so we relied on by word of mouth to find where individuals had taken refuge and determine what sort of losses they had suffered, and then compiled the results in lists.

As we tried to find members, it was a joy to meet old friends again and exchange words of thanks that we had made it through the disaster safely. Such meetings were joyous occasions. It was a time when the simple act of seeing someone could be a moving experience.

I went to Kesennuma Center to check on the condition of the hall. The tsunami submerged it to above the second story level. All of the hall's equipment was ruined, and the building was beyond salvage.

the March 16, 2011 issue of the Seikyo Shimbun carried a message from Honorary President Daisaku Ikeda.

From the moment the quake subsided, the hearts of those of us who jumped into relief efforts were nearly overwhelmed by feelings of resignation and helplessness in the face of nature's irresistible fury, as well as fatigue and anxiety arising out of inability to imagine what the future might possibly hold in store. Against this, President Ikeda's words of encouragement buoyed the spirits of members and helped them find strength to look to the future: "Nothing can destroy the treasures of the heart." "I am offering solemn prayers for all your loved ones — family members and friends — who have lost their lives. This disaster is truly heartbreaking. Life, however, is eternal, and through chanting daimoku, we can transcend life and death to connect with the lives of those who have passed away." "Never be defeated! Have courage! Have hope!"

In rendering assistance to Kesennuma, we concentrated on distributing relief supplies to people who were sheltering in their homes. Thanks to the familiarity of long-time residents with the area, we were able to identify many people living in isolation in more remote neighborhoods, and delivered relief supplies to them as well.

Presently, people began asking us for help with clearing rubble and such, so we started providing support in that

the Tohoku Culture Center includes managing Gakkai facilities within the prefecture.

By the fourth day after the earthquake, we still could not determine the status of the Kesennuma Center, so I decided to go there to check it.

Because of road damage and other problems, getting there took five hours, about twice the normal time. I tried taking a route that runs adjacent to the rail line, but it was blocked by rubble.

Frustrated, I decided to go to Tome City, about an hour and a half's drive from Kesennuma, and set up a relief support headquarters for Kesennuma at the center there. There I spent the next month, working days and nights at the center to support the people of Kesennuma.

In the days following the earthquake, I was often assailed by feelings of helplessness as the true scale of the disaster became apparent.

Why did this happen in the Tohoku region? Why did the people living there, and our own fellow members, have to undergo such suffering? Why did so many people have to lose beloved members of their families?

The outrageous reality of the disaster often made me feel like my heart would burst, and I shed many tears as I often felt that my spirit would break.

As these feelings of hopelessness were reaching a peak,

atmosphere became inescapably noisome.

We also had to maintain a healthy environment inside the center. Because the disaster occurred during the cold season, we made maximum use of sanitary masks and alcohol as measures to avoid spreading cold and influenza viruses.

Starting on the third day of the crisis, we began posting a daily schedule, including daily activities such as breakfast, radio exercises, ventilation, and cleaning.

Among the refugees were people who had escaped the tsunami, as well as people who didn't know if their family members were dead or alive. They were all very anxious. We therefore took every opportunity to extend words of encouragement.

With greetings of "Good morning!" and "How do you feel today?" we would open the curtains and hold radio exercises. Our hope was that by giving people an opportunity to speak, they could dispel in some small way feelings that were pent up inside. Then, asking for help from members who were nurses and doctors, we began holding health consultations.

The joy of meeting old friends

Besides supporting organization activities, my job at

in 2004 and the Chuetsu Offshore Earthquake in 2007, the members in Niigata knew what was needed and did not wait to be asked before arranging for shuttle shipments of emergency supplies such as fuel oil, drinking water, bread, and portable toilets.

Everyone at the center had moist eyes as we read handwritten messages that were included with handmade rice balls of varying shapes and sizes: "Never give up!" "Hang in there." "We're praying for you. Let's get through this together."

The supplies and messages came from all over the country, and the warmth of feeling that accompanied them helped support us when we had reached our limits of physical and mental endurance.

Along with food, sanitation was a tremendous problem. Although the center had a stock of portable toilets for emergency use, most refugees had no idea how to use them. Therefore, staff members equipped with flashlights and wearing jackets against the cold took turns waiting at the entrances to washrooms. Explanations about how to use the emergency facilities had to be provided around the clock.

I can't adequately express my appreciation to the members who showed such dedication, saying "Anything to help the victims" as they took turns in an area where the

them to eat the next day.

We had some pre-washed rice in the staff cafeteria. Neighborhood Gakkai members provided us with eight household rice cookers, and we used these to cook rice for rice balls. However, the amount of rice you can cook in a household rice cooker is very limited; only about enough for fifteen rice balls. In the meantime, the number of people taking refuge in the center was growing steadily.

Using the rice cookers and the center's emergency power supply, the management and staff of the center worked throughout the night together with local members to prepare food for the next day. As a result, by the next morning we had about a thousand small rice balls ready, which were sufficient for the moment.

Gakkai groups in neighboring prefectures quickly stepped in with help. At 2 a.m. the next morning, just twelve hours after the quake, the first shipment of emergency relief supplies arrived from the Soka Gakkai in Yamagata Prefecture. The carriers succeeded in delivering the supplies despite having to wend their way through a road network that had been shredded by the earthquake. Thanks to that effort, the next morning we were able to supplement the rice balls with water, sausage and such.

Later that same day, 5,500 rice balls arrived from Niigata Prefecture. Having experienced the Chuetsu Earthquake

March 11, 2011: More Than Survival

The first refugees started arriving at the Tohoku Culture Center about twenty minutes after the earthquake. These were followed by many other people from the surrounding area, and by 11 p.m., the number of refugees in the center had swelled to more than three hundred.

In the end, the Tohoku Culture Center extended shelter to a thousand refugees, while the fourteen centers in Miyagi Prefecture together took in three thousand, and the forty-two Gakkai centers gave shelter to up to about five thousand.

The Tohoku Culture Center served as a refugee shelter for about a month and a half. During this time, our focus in running the center was to provide maximum protection for the health and safety of those who came to us for shelter.

However, we were severely challenged by the interruption of electricity, gas, and water services, as well as inability to expect any relief supplies from the authorities. This made assuring the safety and security of refugees a challenge of great magnitude, and meeting that challenge took all our efforts.

The first problem was food. It wasn't until after 11 p.m. on the day of the quake that we hit on a way of providing our three hundred refugees with some food the next morning. Until then, we had no idea what we would give

Refugee support began immediately after the quake

"Will the building collapse? Will I die here?"

Those thoughts ran through my head as I sat through shaking more violent than anything I'd ever experienced.

When the Great East Japan Earthquake and Tsunami struck on March 11, 2011, I was at work in the Soka Gakkai Tohoku Culture Center in Sendai City. The three minutes of shaking seemed to go on forever.

As the trembling finally started subsiding, alarm lamps lit on machines everywhere and buzzers started sounding. "We need to set up a disaster relief headquarters!", I shouted, and immediately got in touch with the Soka Gakkai's headquarters in Tokyo by telephone. Starting with the boilers, we began inspecting the center's equipment and checking for injuries among people in the building.

At the time, I was one of the leaders of the Youth Division of the Soka Gakkai in Miyagi Prefecture, so I began working with my colleagues to determine conditions at other centers within the prefecture. However, our efforts to contact other centers failed. I later found out that the centers at Kesennuma and Ishinomaki had been swallowed up by the tsunami.

March 11, 2011: More Than Survival

"Network of encouragement" in the wake of the 2011 Great East Japan Earthquake and Tsunami

After the quake, many survivors found shelter at Soka Gakkai centers. Youth Division members and many others worked around the clock in support of disaster response efforts.

Senior Youth Division Leader, Tohoku Soka Gakkai
Mikio Yamane

(laughs).

Kaneji: I think the bonds we share are especially strong because of the difficulties we have overcome together. I want us to keep on encouraging each other as we move ahead together.

Kaneji: After a while, I received word that my company was reopening, so in the latter part of April, I returned to our house by myself. The town was still mostly uninhabited, and for some reason it seems the birds had deserted it too. Hungry dogs would follow me around, and it was a very creepy feeling.

My workplace was a complete mess, and I spent days from morning to night just cleaning up. When we finally finished after four months, everyone gave a big cheer.

Kiyoko: While the two of us were able to return home, there are many people who can't return even though they want to. I have friends who have taken refuge all over the country, but I still keep in touch with them.

Kaneji: The refugees of the nuclear accident hold a gathering called the "Utsukushima Phoenix Group" where we get together periodically for mutual encouragement. The first gathering was held in June, just three months after the disaster, but I was so happy to see people again that tears came to my eyes and I couldn't speak.

Kiyoko: That's right. Just seeing peoples' faces was a comfort, and made me feel much better. There was much clasping of hands and rejoicing at getting together again.

Thereafter, we've held gatherings in Tokyo, Fukushima and so forth, and each time someone comments about how their tear ducts have loosened up since the disaster

expression and making people laugh.

Kaneji: Each morning, I would announce, "Ta-dah! I will now introduce today's breakfast menu! Today we have rice balls made of premium Akita rice and fully ripe bananas! And Suntory beer! Oh wait, it's Suntory water!" That would generally get a laugh and lighten things up.

Kiyoko: I can say this now, but there were times when putting on a smiling face seemed like an impossibility. But I reasoned that looking cheerful would help give hope to others, so I never let up while I was with people.

Kaneji: The Gakkai hall was not an official refugee center, so it was closed after about ten days. Before closing the hall, we met with each of the refugees individually and asked them where they would be going next. Based on their answers, we made arrangements to give each quantities of gasoline sufficient to reach their destinations and we sent them on their way.

After leaving the Peace Center, the Kanazawas' took shelter for a while with their daughter in Kanagawa Prefecture, but before long they rented an apartment in Iwaki, after which they returned to Hironomachi once the evacuation order was lifted. However, nearly half of the evacuees from the town are still unable to return to their homes.

March 11, 2011: More Than Survival

Kept smiling to cheer others

Kiyoko: Our first priority was securing food. We asked Gakkai friends in the neighborhood for help, and they provided rice and vegetables and loaned us rice cookers, which helped us make ends meet for a while.

The first thing we made was rice gruel. Although we could only give each person about half a paper cup full, within two or three days we started receiving relief supplies from members all over the country. We were so grateful.

Kaneji: There were about a hundred and thirty refugees at the Peace Hall, including both Gakkai members and non-members. The day after we arrived, the refugees were divided into communal living teams, including a cleaning team, a cooking team, a water fetching team, and so forth. Thankfully, we also had some people who were very good at cooking, as well as a toilet specialist who was versed in odor control, a nurse, and people with other valuable skills.

Kiyoko: We gave a lot of attention to maintaining a positive mood in the hall. Everyone there was worried about the future, and it would have been easy to let the mood turn dark. So, hoping to keep the atmosphere as light as possible, I put effort into keeping a cheerful

However, no information was given as to why we should evacuate, or where we were supposed to go.

Kaneji: The first thing I did was go out and look at the wind direction. Since the wind was blowing from south to north, we decided to head south.

Kiyoko: We headed for our family home in Iwaki to take temporary refuge there. However, along the way we received a telephone call from a fellow Soka Gakkai member who told us that many people had taken refuge in the Iwaki Culture Center. I was previously an official of the Gakkai's regional organization, so rather than head for the family home, we decided to go to the Iwaki Culture Center.

Kaneji: By the time we arrived, around thirty or forty people had taken refuge in the hall.

Kiyoko: Soon thereafter, an order was given to evacuate an area close to the Iwaki Culture Center, so on the same day we moved to the Iwaki Peace Center, which is further from the nuclear plant.

Kaneji: The roads were bumpy and filled with traffic, and I don't remember how we did it, but somehow or another we made it to the Peace Center.

Kiyoko: It was very cold that day, but the Iwaki Peace Center had electricity, and we greatly appreciated the warmth inside.

tsunami came, we would be trapped by water entering the building, so we all moved to a high spot inside the grounds of the facility.

We had just reached the high spot when water started receding from the sea front, and soon we could see the sea floor of a fishing spot located near the plant. Presently, a pitch black sheet of water came rushing in, which looked like a huge iron plate. It was like watching a movie, it all seemed so unreal.

The tsunami came in seven waves. Biggest by far was the second wave, and it washed all sorts of things around inside the power plant.

My car was washed away, so that evening I wound up walking four kilometers to get back to my house.

The following day, March 12, there was a great hydrogen explosion in the containment building of Unit 1 at the Fukushima Daiichi Nuclear Power Station. Although the Kanazawas' hometown of Hironomachi is located twenty to thirty kilometers from the plant, on March 13 the population of the entire town was ordered to evacuate.

Kiyoko: During the evening of the 12th, the town's loudspeakers started broadcasting, "Evacuate the town," which at that point was a request for voluntary evacuation.

Quick-thinking decision to evacuate to high ground

Kiyoko: When the earthquake hit, I was visiting my friend in the city of Iwaki. The quake's shaking was intense, greater than any I'd ever experienced, and though we all ran outside in a panic, there was nothing to hang on to, so we wound up standing with our arms wrapped around each other's shoulders until the shaking subsided.

Going into the city, we saw manholes with their covers blown off and shattered streets everywhere. Soon after, I heard that a tsunami was coming, so I took a route on the hillward side of the city to head home.

Along the way, I picked up a woman who was standing in the road soaking wet. Her car had been swept away by the tsunami, and she barely escaped with her life. Unbelievable things were happening one after another.

Kaneji: I was doing construction work at a thermal power plant in Hironomachi. This plant is located about twenty kilometers from the Fukushima Daiichi nuclear plant, and when the earthquake struck I was changing oil on the first floor of the No. 5 West building.

Thinking the place I was in wasn't safe, I first took refuge with some workers from another company in the building's basement. However, we soon realized that if a

March 11, 2011: More Than Survival

Helped care for refugees following the disaster, built congenial rapport and bonds of fellowship

The Kanazawas live in Hironomachi, a town located within thirty kilometers of the Fukushima Daiichi Nuclear Power Station. Although the couple were forced to evacuate after the nuclear accident, they provided constant support and encouragement to others in the days following.

Kaneji Kanazawa

Kiyoko Kanazawa

(Hironomachi, Fukushima Prefecture)

to become an oasis for these people. Living in cramped temporary housing is not easy, and many people live alone. I would like it to become a place where people can come to laugh and make jokes.

Sakae: I feel thankful that many people have said, "I hope you never stop running the restaurant here." As long as we have such customers, I want to keep the restaurant open.

At the same time, when the evacuation order on Iitatemura is lifted and people start returning to their former home, I would like to reopen "Chuka Kohaku" in Iitatemura as well.

Since there are concerns about radiation, and many people have lived in a different place for a long time, there will probably be many who will never return. In spite of that, I do want to reopen the restaurant in Iitatemura. For me, that will be giving back to the community.

I want to keep the spirit of "never give up" and work on behalf of Iitatemura's recovery.

So I began looking for a place where we could reopen the restaurant in the city where we took refuge.

Toshiko: But finding a suitable place wasn't that easy. Whenever we saw a place that looked right, it would be too expensive. Then just as we were about to give up, the administration of Iitatemura asked if we would be interested in opening a restaurant in Fukushima City's temporary housing project.

Although the building is a modular structure, we didn't have to pay for construction, and we were offered assistance for three quarters of the opening expenses. That gave us reason to be grateful that we had experienced so much difficulty with finding a place on our own!

The new "Chuka Kohaku" opened in November, 2011.

Sakae: The temporary housing project where we opened the restaurant houses about 500 people, and all of them were refugees from Iitatemura. Among them were many of our former patrons, and we thought that it would be great if we could get them and former neighbors to come. So we were staggered when three hundred customers came to the restaurant on opening day! We even had a line form outside. Folk were truly happy to see our restaurant reopen, some saying the sight of our shop sign brought tears to their eyes.

Toshiko: It would make me very happy for our restaurant

well, and could only leave ourselves after everyone else was gone. We didn't have time to think about ourselves while taking care of the villagers and the refugees.

There were three people who could not be convinced to leave the village, and we had to go back to talk to them again and again.

We didn't see this as a great ordeal, it was just a matter of having to do things as they came up.

Subsequently, the Akaishizawas moved into housing that was rented by the prefecture in Iizakamachi, Fukushima.

Sakae: I've only been back to Iitatemura once since the evacuation. At that time it hit me that an uninhabited town is a very lonely place. Not only that, but it is located amongst the mountains, and is without power or any other services. It is truly a terrible sight. Looking at that little world that we once lived in, one gets a feeling of how happy lives can be destroyed in an instant, and overwhelmed with darkness. It is a world without light.

I stopped by our restaurant and found frying pans and pots in disarray around the inside of the shop. However, the dishware that we put away properly was mostly undamaged. When I saw that, the thought that welled up inside me was, "We can start over! I'm not giving up!"

whatsoever to spare for with outsiders. Those who wanted to go on from Iitatemura to other refugee centers couldn't do so for lack of fuel. No matter how much they pleaded, there was nothing we could do.

Sakae: But people would come to us crying with their children. So we ended up giving them our own ration tickets.

Reopens restaurant at evacuation housing project

April 11 when one month passed from the day of the earthquake. Then an evacuation order was issued for five municipalities outside the 20-kilometer radius from Fukushima Daiichi, including Iitatemura.

Toshiko: Iitatemura is located about forty kilometers from the Fukushima Daiichi power plants, so when our evacuation order was issued, at first I couldn't feel that it was real. There was no change in the appearance of the village, and I just thought, why should we evacuate?

Sakae: At that time, I and other members of the fire department were putting our own needs second as we gave priority to refugees who had evacuated to Iitatemura. Then we had to evacuate the residents of Iitatemura as we had no idea about how serious it actually was.

Then the telephone rang, and we heard that we would be receiving thousands of refugees. From then, it was like being in a war zone.

Toshiko: At first, Iitatemura was not included in the exclusion zone. Instead, we began receiving many refugees from Minamisoma and other coastal towns.

Sakae: So many cars came that roads were completely blocked, and nothing could move. We took turns working around the clock to receive all these people. The number who evacuated to Iitatemura reached 4,000. I was the assistant chief of the village's fire department, so preparing for the refugees and telling them where to go kept me very busy.

The public hall and gymnasium were pressed into service as emergency shelters, and the people of the village brought space heaters and blankets for the refugees from their own houses. The women of the village worked three shifts to prepare food, and morning, noon and evening walked around distributing 4,000 rice balls to people. People brought all of the food that they had in their pantries.

Toshiko: The biggest problem was the lack of gasoline. Deliveries to the village stopped altogether. Villagers received ration tickets good for 10 liters, but we had none

them out in the neighborhood along with pickles and the like.

Sakae: A rumor started that we had begun running a soup kitchen at my place, and I had to tell them that was wrong, I'm just passing these out in the neighborhood (laughs). Although the power was stopped, our rice cooker was an industrial gas-powered model, so we were able to cook rice. So I told them, "If you bring us the rice, we'll cook it for you."

Fortunately, the restaurant was unharmed. As it happened, we had finished renovating the shop shortly before the earthquake, and we had reinforcing columns installed at the time. So we thought, "If we just clean up inside, we can reopen for business. We've been protected."

However, not long thereafter, the couple's life was completely disrupted by the accident at the Fukushima Daiichi Nuclear Power Station. Iitatemura is located almost entirely outside a 30-kilometer radius centered on Fukushima Daiichi, so at first it was not included in the evacuation zone, and it received refugees from other areas.

Sakae: While watching news about the disaster on TV with the village chief at the public hall, we were sorry to hear about the extent of the destruction, but at the time

Helped refugees prepare their food

The Akaishizawas first opened "Chuka Kohaku" in 1977. The restaurant was a favorite among residents of Iitatemura for over thirty years. However, the couple's life changed on March 11, 2011, following the Great East Japan Earthquake.

Toshiko: On that day, I and my husband were working in the restaurant, just like always. The instant the quake stuck, I was knocked to my knees, and instinctively grasped at a customer's legs (laughs).

My husband quickly jumped out the front of the restaurant to help some children. There is a school bus stop in front of the shop, and many children who'd just gotten off the bus were gathered out front when the quake started.

Sakae: The shaking was so violent that the road was undulating. When I thought about the children in front of the shop, I forgot all about my wife and customers (laughs), and leapt to their assistance. I quickly yelled at them to gather together and guided them to a nearby plaza. There was also a pregnant lady with a small child in the group.

Toshiko: The quake knocked out the power, but we made rice balls using what rice we had in the shop and passed

March 11, 2011: More Than Survival

Unbroken by nuclear disaster, reopens shop at evacuation housing project, energizing people of home town

Sakae Akaishizawa and his wife of many years, Toshiko, made their living as operators of the "Chuka Kohaku" Chinese restaurant in Iitatemura, Fukushima Prefecture. Although they were forced to evacuate following the accident at the Fukushima Daiichi Nuclear Power Station, their fighting spirit would not admit defeat, and they later opened up a new restaurant. This has become a haven for people from their old hometown.

Sakae Akaishizawa
Toshiko Akaishizawa

(Iitatemura, Fukushima Prefecture)

Yuko: Several years have now passed since the disaster, and day by day, the feeling grows that "We must make sure that no one else ever has to suffer from such an experience." At the same time, through this experience we also came to feel that human beings are capable of strength and kindness even under the most extreme circumstances.

Yoshihiro: That is very true. While we witnessed the terrible power of nature, we also saw that the power of people is amazing.

Our house is located twenty-one kilometers from the Fukushima Daiichi Nuclear Power Station, just a short distance outside of the 20-kilometer evacuation zone. It is, so to speak, the "front line," but I believe there is meaning in living in this place. While we are still feeling our way, I am confident that we will continue advancing.

off, and hung up laundry indoors to dry.

Sheltering indoors divides people from each other, resulting in isolation. When you think about radiation under such circumstances, you come to fear death. That makes the experience we had of getting back together with friends in the area an unforgettable experience.

Today, Minamisoma City is divided into areas where it is expected that the residents have difficulties in returning for a long time, areas in which the residents are not permitted to live, areas to which evacuation orders are ready to be lifted, and areas where people can come and go as they please. Both people who have stayed in Minamisoma and those who have moved elsewhere suffer from various feelings.

Yoshihiro: The other day, a meeting was held to make decisions about reconstruction in Minamisoma, and many people who formerly lived in the area hurried to join in. They all looked very happy to be meeting old friends again.

Watching their expressions and manner, I thought, "The people who have remained, and those who have started new lives elsewhere, all of them have missions." Even though some live elsewhere, it is the connections of the heart that matter most.

force, and the high school's gymnasium was pressed into service as a mortuary. Ultimately, facilities at a school located outside the 30-kilometer radius were borrowed, and our children started going to school by bus every morning.

Yuko: That one school building was shared between several schools. For example, the first floor was used by one elementary school, and the second floor was used by another. I heard that lunches were very simple because the lunch center was also providing meals for the evacuation center, and they usually consisted of just a couple of rice balls wrapped in cellophane, a stick of cheese fish paste, and milk.

Under the circumstances, some children transferred to other schools. When their friends transferred, our kids would come home depressed. That made things hard on their parents as well.

Yoshihiro: Subsequently, the school's graduation ceremony was held at the original facility, and the evacuation of the school ended in February of the following year.

Yuko: Looking back, it very trying living entirely indoors and trying to trying to minimize circulation to keep radiation out. We didn't even use the ventilation fans when we were cooking or bathing. We kept the air conditioner

order remained in effect until April 22.

Yuko: We stayed at our friend's house for eleven days. Then when we went back to check our house in Minamisoma on March 26, our children said, "we absolutely want to stay here!" I think that the insecurity of staying in an unfamiliar place weighed on them heavily.

Yoshihiro: And at that point, we made up our minds that we would stay at our house in Minamisoma, and live while taking shelter indoors.

The strength people show in dire straits

Yuko: While some people evacuated Minamisoma, others stayed behind. In either case, it was a difficult decision.

Yoshihiro: At first, very little in the way of relief supplies made it into the "shelter indoors" area, and we would stand in line for up to two hours to get bread and canned food.

Yuko: We received notice that the schools our children attended would be closed in March, and then the closure was extended through April. Then we were suddenly informed that we should evacuate, and submit requests for transfer to other schools. We were stunned.

Yoshihiro: The gymnasium of our elementary school was transformed into a outpost of the national self defense

public toilets, so we decided not to evacuate in haste.

Then on the evening of the 14th, we heard on the news that pressure was building up inside the Unit 2 reactor's containment vessel. However, residents did not receive any information about this from the local authorities.

And then we started receiving text messages like, "Heading inland now, almost no residents left," and "We are leaving soon too. Thanks for everything." We began to wonder, "Should we be staying here?"

Yoshihiro: In the end, we wound up evacuating Minamisoma at about 6 a.m. on the 15th, and the explosion at the Unit 2 reactor was reported shortly thereafter. I think we were just in the nick of time.

Yuko: So off we went, with my 88-year-old father-in-law and our three children, heading where we didn't know. We thought there wouldn't be any stores open, so we took along what food and spices we had in the house, together with water and so forth.

Waking up our sleeping children, we fashioned masks of wet handkerchiefs, covered their heads with disaster hoods, and started heading single-mindedly north.

Yoshihiro: We wound up taking refuge in the home of a friend in Soma City. The day we evacuated, the area wihin a radius of twenty to thirty kilometers of the nuclear plant was declared a "shelter indoors" area. The "shelter indoors"

hall.

The area was crowded with young people who were bringing supplies. Seeing them, I thought "Well, there's hope for Japan yet."

At the time of the earthquake, the Matsumoto family were all in different locations, but they were all safe. However, their relief was soon shattered, as the accident at the Fukushima Daiichi Nuclear Power Station ushered in a life accompanied by constant fear of radiation.

Yuko: Immediately after the nuclear power plant accident, confusion reigned, and the authorities couldn't decide what to do, first ordering residents to shelter indoors, and then later canceling the order. On the 12th, one day after the quake, an order was issued to evacuate all residents from within a 20-kilometer radius of the nuclear power plant.

Yoshihiro: At the time, we weren't sure whether our house was inside the 20-kilometer radius, so we stayed put. We later found out that our house is located about twenty-one kilometers from the plant.

Yuko: We received text messages from people who did evacuate telling of roads that were so crowded they couldn't get out of their driveways, and of long lines at

Choosing to continue living at home

Yuko: When the earthquake struck, I was away from home. My husband was at work, my son Takuya and youngest daughter, Maki, were at school, and my oldest daughter, Yumi, was at home with her grandfather. The shaking was so severe that I was sure my house must have collapsed!

I tried phoning my husband many times, but I couldn't get through to him. I was starting to feel frantic, but told myself to stay calm and went to the elementary school to pick up my younger daughter.

Yoshihiro: I immediately headed straight home. When I got there, I found my older daughter and her grandfather waiting outside. They were afraid to go back in the house.

Yuko: I drove home with my younger daughter, and when my older daughter saw my face, she burst into tears.

Yoshihiro: She was afraid that her mother had been swept away in the tsunami. Later, my son came home from high school, and we had all the family safely together again.

Yuko: I think it was about 11 p.m. that night that we heard over the disaster warning system "There is a shortage of living supplies and food at refugee centers." Thinking "This is no time to be stingy," I gathered up what blankets and rice balls we had in the house and took them to the city

March 11, 2011: More Than Survival

Continuing life near the border of the evacuation zone

The home of the Matsumoto family is located about twenty-one kilometers from the Fukushima Daiichi Nuclear Power Station. Although many people have left, the Matsumoto family has deep roots in the area and pursues happiness and reconstruction in their original home.

Yoshihiro Matsumoto

Yuko Matsumoto

(Minamisoma City, Fukushima Prefecture)

Sunflowers," when children asked about the meaning of "generation 50," I could use them to tell them the story of the 2011 Great East Japan Earthquake and Tsunami. So the "Gallant Sunflowers" may become "messengers of tradition" for telling about the earthquake and natural disaster.

Now the gallant sunflowers have reached their sixth generation. I think of the successive generations as ticks marking the passage of time.

With the cooperation of many people, the "Gallant Sunflowers" of Ishinomaki have become messengers of hope and friendship to India, China, America, England, Brazil, France, Italy and other countries around the world.

Presently, I am working through a civic group called the "Pull together! Ishinomaki" association which I founded. The group promotes events and activities such as leaving memorials at the "Pull together! Ishinomaki" billboard, traditionalizing the stories of the disaster for children, and using the "Gallant Sunflowers" to build traditions for transmission to the future.

Together with our many friends, we will go on "pulling together" for the sake of Ishinomaki and the surrounding region.

March 11, 2011: More Than Survival

for them, and they rapidly grew and soon produced magnificent sunflower blossoms.

We were astonished. The sludge that flowed into the area made it hard for even summer weeds to grow. Who would have thought that sunflowers could grow in a place that was inhospitable to weeds?

Several months after the disaster, the mental and physical fatigue of recovery work had reached a peak. Finding the sunflowers at just that time was a big boost. Seeing them growing valiantly in salt-contaminated ground made me think, "If sunflowers can do it, so can I."

I started calling these blooms the "Gallant Sunflowers," and began posting updates on their progress through social media. The responses I received showed that this gave joy to many people.

Ken'ichi Kurosawa packaged up the sunflower seeds ten to a bag and gave them to people as tokens of gratitude and appreciation. Many of those people took joy in planting those seeds in their own homes. Ken'ichi says that impressed him with the "Gallant Sunflower's" power.

Thinking to pass the "Gallant Sunflowers" on to the future, I started naming them by generation. The idea was that once I'd reached the 50th generation of "Gallant

casualties.

I think that people just picked the spot as a place where they could deposit their feelings.

Truth be told, before erecting the billboard, I was conflicted about whether I should do so. I wondered whether it was appropriate to put up such a structure at a time when people were still suffering even from lack of sufficient food.

But while I was putting up the sign, an old neighborhood fellow told me, "That's the way to do it! I'm pulling too!" That made me feel that the sign had meaning.

For some people, the words "Pull together" are still hard to deal with. While I recognize that some people feel that way, I want to keep putting the message out there.

"Gallant Sunflowers" as a "messenger of tradition"

Thinking that I'd like to bring some color back to the town, which had been reduced to colorless rubble, I planted some flower seedlings around the billboard.

One day while watering the flowers and cutting back weeds around the billboard, my wife found some stray sunflowers growing next to the sign. I think they sprouted from seeds deposited by the tsunami. We started caring

possessions were gone along with people we loved, and everything seemed hopeless.

Seeing this, I thought that I had to do something, and I asked myself what I as a survivor could do.

The lot where my house once stood faced a road, and the location was visible from the Hiyoriyama refugee center, so I hit upon the idea of erecting a billboard to boost people's spirits.

After collecting pieces of plywood that had been dropped by the receding waters, I asked a carpenter friend to help me erect the sign. Then I got together with two friends, and the three of us painted the words, "Pull together! Ishinomaki" on the sign. We painted the word "Ishinomaki" in blue because, even though it had been devastated by the tsunami, it was still a town of the sea.

That was just a month after the earthquake. The big sign they built from wreckage and debris measures 1.8 meters in height and stretches 10.8 meters in width, and after it was picked up by the media, it became a symbol of reconstruction that attracted attention even from abroad.

By and by, people began laying flowers by the billboard. At first I thought this was strange, but Miyagi Prefecture's Ishinomaki city incurred a tremendous cost in human

area was shrouded in clouds. That was smoke from fires. Shouting my wife's name, I continued walking through the muddy water. But my voice was drowned out by the rotor noise from a circling helicopter.

Waves of fear and anxiety poured over me.

Because of the fires, I couldn't reach my house. "It's hopeless," I thought, "she might be gone." My tears wouldn't stop.

But I didn't stop looking, and after searching all day, I finally found her, alive, at the Hiyoriyama refugee center. When I saw her, my legs gave way and I collapsed to the floor. I couldn't speak at all.

Mrs. Kurosawa says that her house half collapsed when it was struck by another house being carried along in the torrent. Amidst the wreckage of walls and roof, she stood in the ruin of her second floor room until she was rescued from the midst of the flood before sunset.

Erected a billboard: "Pull together! Ishinomaki"

Following the disaster, everyone was depressed as we looked for missing family or the remnants of our homes. A search for bodies got underway, and the dead were lined up wrapped in blankets as they were found. Our

March 11, 2011: More Than Survival

I thought, "I can't stay here," so I abandoned the car and climbed a tree. However, the tree's thin branches snapped under my weight, and I fell down head first. Scrambling back up the bank, I jumped into a pine tree and climbed for my life. Immediately below, the tsunami was flowing past at a fearsome rate, and the height of the water was steadily rising.

Shrubbery and vehicles floated by. I saw another person clinging to a tree just like me, but presently he disappeared. I thought he was probably swept away.

From the tree, I was able to reach my wife once by phone, but she just said, "I'm at home," and then I lost the connection.

Snow started falling, and it began to get dark. I could hear people screaming and calling for help in the distance, but there was nothing whatsoever that I could do. I clung to that tree throughout the night.

When morning came, I got down from the tree and started walking home. The rows of houses that had been there the day before were all gone, and the whole area was submerged in water. It was just like a lake. Walking through water that came up to my knees, I walked on and on. I couldn't see through the water, and I repeatedly fell into ditches and manholes.

Looking in the direction of my home, it seemed the

Survived the night by clinging to a pine tree

On the day of the quake, I was in Higashimatsushima, the city just to the southwest of Ishinomaki. The terrifying shaking went on and on, and I remember the building across the street swaying like a bowl of jelly, so much that I thought it would topple onto me.

Once the shaking subsided, I tried to return home, which was also my business place. I worked in the piping business, and it occurred to me that my services might be of help in restoring vital lifelines.

Heading for Ishinomaki in my car, I received a call from my wife. She said she was out of the house, but was heading home. I told her "OK, so am I." Immediately after that, the tsunami warning sounded. I tried calling my wife back to tell her to run, but I couldn't reach her no matter how many times I tried. All I could think of was getting to her, and I didn't pause.

The opposite lane was jammed with fleeing vehicles, but I kept going up the coast road. Then ahead I saw something that looked like a barricade. At first I thought it was a no-entry sign, but looking closer I saw it was a car being carried along by the tsunami. I made a hurried U-turn and tried to flee, but found the tsunami was coming at me from the other direction too. I was trapped.

March 11, 2011: More Than Survival

A billboard, "Pull together! Ishinomaki," and building connections through "Gallant Sunflowers"

"Pull together! Ishinomaki" and the billboard that Ken'ichi Kurosawa erected on the site of his former home have become a symbol of reconstruction. "Gallant Sunflowers" sprouting next to the billboard have become messengers carrying an unforgettable reminder of the disaster to the world.

Ken'ichi Kurosawa

(Ishinomaki City, Miyagi Prefecture)

will contribute to the growth of these young people and development of a sense of mission.

Now, in 2016, nearly five years after the disaster, we are undertaking a new project in cooperation with regional producers which aims to make new products and services available to overseas markets. More specifically, we have created a network that includes overseas creators, and beside selling Tohoku products overseas, we are distributing publicity aimed at enticing tourists from overseas to come to Tohoku. To start with, this coming March we plan to introduce products at a festival in Hawaii.

It is with gratitude that I make this report of the progress that has been made in the Tohoku region to the people from around the world who have contributed so generously of their support from the time immediately following the disaster.

overseas and in the Tohoku region, Ken Matsuda speaks of his renewed impressions of Japanese culture and the strength of the people of Tohoku.

Japan is blessed with a well-developed infrastructure, as well as many outstanding people with a high level of social awareness. Such people are found not only in international cooperation organizations like our own, but increasingly in humanitarian assistance groups that run under the auspices of government, volunteer groups, and private industry.

However, Japan is an aging society, and so the number of young people is decreasing. And that, I think, is the challenge.

Developing countries lack social safety nets and well-developed infrastructure, making conditions very difficult. However, they have many young people. Despite the poor conditions, the eyes of children shine. And there is where I feel the future.

Of course, we have also encountered many bright young children in the Tohoku disaster area. We've even met children who tell stories about funny experiences they had in the midst of their trying life as refugees. We've also met children who express appreciation for the efforts being made by adults. I am sure that all such positive memories

due to the disaster, the supermarkets had no choice but to switch to other suppliers. Consequently, processing companies do not have sales channels available even if they rebuild. So, we opened up an online shop together with a marine product processing company, and created a new brand for direct sale to customers.

In forming such teams, one of the issues we encountered was differences in perception between management teams of different generations. Many serving company presidents are in their seventies, and even when younger-generation folk in their twenties and thirties think of new approaches, the older generation tends to want to rely on their own experience when rebuilding. Moreover, many of these company presidents are veteran survivors of turbulent times and have very sharp instincts.

Under such circumstances, starting up a new business requires making various compromises. So, we joined up with the management teams of such companies to combine hands and brains in undertaking challenges together.

Now we "escort" the people who are responsible for the regional economy and work together with them on developing quality products and marketing them widely.

Based on his experience with support activities both

March 11, 2011: More Than Survival

obtain them.

However, it is really difficult to visualize recovery in the medium and long term. Never before has the world seen such a huge disaster in a developed country in an area with an aging population. As this went beyond all our experience, we didn't have any ready answers. And so, we took each day as it came, fumbling our way as best we could.

For medium to long-term support, I think it is important to discuss problems with local residents and act together with the residents to come up with solutions. To do this, I feel it is important to engage with regional society as "partners," rather than as "supporters."

Therefore, I established a company in Kesennuma which I named "pensea." The mission of this company is to team up with producers in the fields of agriculture, forestry and fisheries, as well as marine product processing companies, providing them with design and marketing support aimed at broadly conveying the appeal of the region's industry.

For example, even if a marine product processing company is reconstructed, it will be faced with a lack of sales channels. This is because while many companies sold processed products to supermarkets before the earthquake, when they were forced to stop operation

Another reason for selecting Kesennuma was that it was a place where support was likely to stall. The transportation backbone of the Tohoku region is made up of the Shinkansen train line and the Tohoku Expressway. Thinking that most support would rely on ground transportation, I reasoned that relief would first reach places that could easily be accessed from these two transportation trunks.

The team I was travelling with discussed the matter, and we decided that we should land in Kesennuma because its location on the coast made it hard to access by land, and it was a place with a sizable population and economy.

Ken Matsuda returned from Indonesia and entered the disaster zone on March 12, the day after the earthquake. With commuters stranded in Tokyo and the nation numb with shock, this was an extraordinarily rapid response.

Cooperation as "partners" rather than as "supporters"

Once we entered Kesennuma, we took measures based on all our previous experience. We made estimates of supplies that would be needed, looking ahead three days, a week, and a month in the future, and made arrangements to

March 11, 2011: More Than Survival

zones and major disaster areas.

When the 2011 Great East Japan Earthquake and Tsunami struck, I was just about to return to Japan from activities in East Timor. I first learned of the earthquake from television while sitting in a dining room in Indonesia. "Oh, how awful," I thought, and hastily made arrangements for return to Japan, hoping to enter the disaster zone as soon as possible.

From previous experience, I know that doing the same things as others during an emergency is liable to result in getting stuck, so I decided to return to Japan by a different route.

The usual route that people take when returning from Indonesia is to enter Japan through Narita airport. Instead, I took a flight that went to Kansai International. From there, I headed for Tokyo by Shinkansen, but wary of becoming stuck at large stations, I got off at Kakegawa Station in Shizuoka Prefecture and headed from there to Tochigi Prefecture by rental car. I knew a place there where I could get a ride on a helicopter.

The place I was flying to was Kesennuma City in Miyagi Prefecture. The destination was determined partly by the helicopter's range. I needed to go as far north as possible and still leave the helicopter with enough fuel for its return trip.

Ken Matsuda

Learned of the disaster while watching TV news in Indonesia

I think it was probably hearing stories my maternal grandfather told when I was very young about his wartime experiences that subconsciously motivated me to become involved in overseas humanitarian assistance activities. The horror of war shocked me, and I think hearing those stories engraved the value of peace deep into my heart.

Growing up, my first job was in general industry, which didn't involve any humanitarian assistance activities at all, but when I saw news of the "9/11" terror attacks that hit America in 2001, I had a strong desire to participate in volunteer activities in New York well up in my heart. I was obsessed by the idea, and contacted various international cooperation organizations, which eventually resulted in a position, but one that involved transporting supplies to Afghanistan.

Although I wound up going to Afghanistan instead of New York, and although that journey wound up lasting for four months rather than the originally scheduled two weeks, the experiences of that time developed into positions with various international cooperation organizations, allowing me to take up support work in war

March 11, 2011: More Than Survival

Taking up the challenge of regional recovery in the aftermath of one of the world's greatest disasters

Ken Matsuda took part in aid programs for refugees and displaced persons in the Middle East, Africa, and various countries in Asia. Following the 2011 Great East Japan Earthquake and Tsunami, he moved to Kesennuma City in the heart of the disaster zone and began assisting with regional recovery and development efforts.

Ken Matsuda

(Kesennuma City, Miyagi Prefecture)

not be "reconstruction." I think that truly "reconstructing the heart" can only be achieved by rediscovering that new person in yourself, and it is from the moment of that discovery that one becomes once again capable of having hopes and dreams.

Though our batting center, I hope to bring many dreams to Kesennuma. And one of the dreams I have now is to establish a sister city relationship between Kesennuma and Tokyo's Chofu City, the place where I was raised.

More than anything, I want to be a "life guide" for my son, the one remaining member of my family. I want him to see a father whose spirit is indomitable, and who will continue pursuing his dreams no matter the troubles encountered along the way.

March 11, 2011: More Than Survival

the city's rebirth from the ashes of disaster. Also, we built the center with seven driving positions, one for each of the lost members of our family.

Kiyohide has a sign on the wall of his room that says, "A hard winter is always followed by a warm spring! Therefore, never lose hope! Never, ever give up!" Whenever hard reality seemed overwhelming, he would look at that sign, repeat its words to himself, and keep on moving.

After losing my family, I became in a way two people, one who was always weeping over misfortune, and another who was always striving mightily. After going on this way for a while, I asked myself, "What would my lost family members have wanted of me?" And in that instant, I realized that they would certainly wish for my happiness.

From the moment of that realization, I decided to quit being a person who wept, and become one who worked and took action on behalf of others. And it was from that moment that my hope was reborn.

People talk about the importance of "reconstructing the heart" alongside "reconstructing the town," but I think "reconstructing the heart" really means searching for a new person in yourself. Going back to the way things were before the disaster might be "restoration," but it would

However, making the determination was one thing. Getting hold of the needed capital and land for construction was quite another. Having only the milk dealership as a source of income, I decided to try creating an original product. After much trial and error, what I came up with was a yogurt product named "Yogurt of hope", wishing it bring hope to Kesennuma!

While I intended to use the profits from this to build the batting center, the money didn't exactly rush in. I held product exhibitions and visited recovery events held around the country, selling the yogurt everywhere I went. After a while, my efforts were taken up by television and newspapers, and I starting receiving orders from all over the country.

Many people helped support construction of the batting center. For one, the operator of a golf driving range said that he was closing his business, and offered to give me his nets and net supports. Another was a civil engineering company in Ibaraki Prefecture that offered to provide dump truck loads of dirt for landscaping, as well as an offer of a land loan. Thanks to support from people around the country, we were finally in a position to begin construction.

Our batting center opened on March 30, 2014. We named it "Kesennuma Phoenix", expressing our hope for

I played baseball while in intermediate and high school, and my son, a Little Leaguer, loved baseball too, so after the quake we played catch together almost every day.

One day, during a break from work, I took my son for a visit to a batting center in Oshu City, Iwate Prefecture. Seeing my son there, dripping with sweat and completely absorbed in hitting the pitches, I thought to myself, "This is it!"

Thereafter, I made the hour and a half-long car trip to the batting center with my son just about every month. As we were on the way home one day, my son said, "It would be great if there were a batting center in Kesennuma. Papa, why don't you build one? I have lots of friends who would love to practice batting, if only they could." And on the spot, without thinking much about it, I said, "OK, I'll do it." I thought it would be easy to buy a pitching machine and set it up on an empty lot with a net.

But as days passed and I buried myself in work, I forgot all about the promise until my son came to me and said, "Papa, when are you going to build it?" And I thought to myself, "He's serious! In all the world, I am the only person he can rely on. If I break that promise, there's no telling how it will affect my son, and I could never forgive myself if I let him down." It was then that I got serious. "I WILL build a batting center in Kesennuma!"

him gradually for when I would have to break the news.

It wasn't until three days before the funeral that I managed to tell my son the truth.

Letting him see the bodies would have been too cruel, so I told him, "Let's just keep the good memories." All he said was, "OK."

The first time my son shed any tears was when we went to the crematorium. There, for the first time, he cried out loud.

Perhaps that released some pent-up grief, for afterwards he put on a brave face and assisted by greeting mourners and guiding them to their seats.

Later, he would not speak of his lost family members, to the point where I wondered whether he had actually forgotten them. Now I think he was trying to be considerate of my feelings.

Promise to build a batting center

After the forty-ninth day memorial service was completed, Kiyohide turned to rebuilding the family milk dealership. It was a new start from zero. At that time, trying to think of a way to give encouragement to his son, he hit upon the idea of building a batting center.

way was given some sugar melted in warm water by the operator of a flower shop. I will never forget how delicious that water was, or how grateful I was to receive it.

Kiyohide's son, who was at the elementary school when the quake struck, was safely evacuated, and father and son were reunited three days after the earthquake. However, nothing was heard of the other seven members of his family, who had tried to escape by car.

It was three weeks later that I received notice from the police of my family's death. When I went to the mortuary, I found all seven of them there, all lined up: my wife and two young daughters, my father- and mother-in-law, and my nephew. They were all found dead in their cars.

When I saw the bodies, I nearly collapsed, but at the same time thought, "I don't have any time for crying." The reality of the earthquake's aftermath was just too overwhelming.

For a long time, I couldn't bring myself to tell my son about our family's deaths. Every time I returned to the evacuation center, I'd tell him, "No word today, they still haven't been found." On the other hand, as we bathed together, I'd tell him, "We have to be ready for the worst, we might never see them again." I was trying to prepare

found a large piece, and clinging to that I managed to hold out until I felt the flow of the tsunami begin to reverse. At that point, I knew that unless I did something, I would be dragged out to sea. Struggling against the current, I managed to thrust my arm into the railing of a bridge just as I was about to hit it, and there I clung, narrowly hanging on to the railing and to life.

After a while, I managed to crawl on top of the bridge. It was about that time that the sun went down. It was very cold, my feet were bare, and then it began to snow. Later, I learned that three of my ribs were broken, but at the time I was much too cold to feel any pain.

Looking for a way to preserve even the slightest warmth, I used a stick to fish a large piece of styrofoam out of the current. I broke this up and stuffed the pieces into my clothes.

I thought that I would die if I fell asleep, so as I shivered on the bridge, I screamed and yelled until, after a while, I lost consciousness. When I awoke, it was morning.

"Ah, I'm still alive," was the thought that ran through my head at that moment. In the same instant I thought, "If only that was all a dream." But when I brushed the snow away from my body and arose, the desolation that met my eyes was beyond all imagining.

I started heading for an evacuation center, and along the

March 11, 2011: More Than Survival

A narrow escape, clinging to a bridge railing

On the day of the earthquake, we were at our family's milk dealership. The shaking was so strong that it knocked me to hands and knees. When the shaking subsided, I sent seven members of the family (everyone except for myself and my son, who was a third-grader in elementary school at the time) off in two cars to take refuge at our house, which is located on high ground.

Not long thereafter, I saw the black waters of the tsunami approaching. In panic, I climbed to the building's second floor, but that was soon swallowed up by the water. Frantically, I climbed out onto the roof, but just as I reached it, the whole building started floating. I had no choice but to cling to the roof and let the current take me where it would. After a while, the roof was torn loose from the building with a screeching sound, and I was thrown out in the black waves. In that instant, I thought, "This is the end."

Nonetheless, I struggled to keep afloat, grasping at pieces of debris but then sinking, only to rise again and grasp at other pieces. This happened time and again. The down jacket I was wearing soon became waterlogged, and as it started to drag me down, I discarded it. The small pieces of debris wouldn't keep me afloat, but presently I

Building a batting center to keep promise to son

After losing seven members of his family to the tsunami, Kiyohide Chiba succeeded in overcoming despair together with his grade-school son. Realizing their dream of building a batting center, father and son are moving forward together toward reconstruction.

Kiyohide Chiba

(Kesennuma City, Miyagi Prefecture)

demonstrate victory in our own lives.

We want to live life each day without regret, so "defeat is not an option"!

the ocean.

Fumiko: After seeing that tsunami, maybe fearing the ocean is the normal reaction. Although not all the boats were destroyed, there are some that haven't been back to sea since the earthquake. And I imagine that even those who've resumed fishing are still struggling internally.

Masahiko: I thought about quitting myself. And I thought that quitting would be the easy thing to do. I agonized greatly about it, but ultimately decided that there was no choice but to pick up again and carry on.

And one reason I returned is that life as a fisherman is really very appealing. The more you work, the more you make, and you get to eat well too (laughs). Freshly caught sea urchin and abalone are really quite delicious! I think being a fisherman is the best work in the world.

Fumiko: And a lot of people have told me, "We'd really like to eat Mr. Murakami's seaweed again." That gives us a big boost.

Masahiko: Just the other day, I took in sixty-one kilograms of abalone. That's my biggest catch since the port opened (laughs).

A catch weighing in at double digits is cause for celebration, so sixty-one kilograms is really something. My seaweed harvests have also been tops.

Fumiko: Even though conditions are difficult, we want to

positive mood.

Masahiko: Because of quake, we met students of an elementary school in Machida City, Tokyo. That led to me wanting to show them a real "Big Catch" flag. So we loaned them the "Big Catch" flag of our own boat, the Eikou Maru.

Fumiko: After our boat sank, the flag was all we had left. The students sent us a video showing a Sports Day meet in which the school used the flag.

Later on, the students came to Rikuzentakata to give us a "Big Catch" flag that they'd made themselves. That was a very welcome gift.

Due to the earthquake, many fishermen have quit the business. Masahiko says that he also considered quitting. But in the end, he purchased a new fishing vessel, named it the "No. 3 Eikou Maru," and went back to the sea.

Masahiko: When I started out as a fisherman a quarter of a century ago, I had twenty-eight fellow fishermen working together. Now that number has dwindled to six.

Part of the problem is that we are all getting old, but a lot of boats were sunk, and there's no telling how much wreckage litters the floor of the ocean.

Then there are some who have quit saying that they fear

removing debris that was scattered around the port. That had to be done, or it wouldn't be possible to go out fishing or to resume farming.

Fumiko: Three days after the earthquake, the Self Defense Force started delivering relief supplies. We were so grateful. Even now, I get tears in my eyes when I think about everything they did.

Masahiko: We also received great assistance from our fellow members of the Soka Gakkai. Many people came to help from Hokkaido, Aomori Prefecture and so forth.

Fumiko: We were keeping a dog, and it was also hard not being able to find anything for it to eat. Learning of that, one of the Soka Gakkai members made a special trip to Tono [a city in central Iwate Prefecture] to buy it food.

There was another young man who, saying he couldn't find words of encouragement, played the harmonica for us.

Masahiko: After the quake, members from Hyogo Prefecture came three times to give us encouragement. They said, "After what we went through in the wake of the Great Hanshin Earthquake, we couldn't just sit by."

Fumiko: Afterwards, we were invited to Hyogo, where we took part in an exchange meeting. After living among mountains of debris, seeing the happy faces of all the members at the bright hall really helped put us in a

Including those who were never found, Rikuzentakata lost 1,700 people to the tsunami, 7.2% of its population. The survivors were faced with a severe battle to begin rebuilding.

Masahiko: Although our house was OK, for quite a while no food was available, and since we gave everything that we had to the neighbors, we had nothing to eat ourselves (laughs).

Fumiko: Our neighbors had lost their houses to the tsunami, and having fled with just the clothes on their backs, we wanted to do for them what we could. Before we knew it, we had given away all of our harvested seaweed and our rice too (laughs).

I just wanted them to have something to eat, so that their bellies would feel better.

Masahiko: The power outage lasted for about two months. The water was out too, so we would bring water from the river in buckets and boil it for hot water, which we used to bathe.

Fumiko: I can tell you that when you eat in the dark, you can't tell what you are eating, and it doesn't taste good.

Encouraged by support from all over the country

Masahiko: Following the quake, I spent the days

a two-storey building floating away, apparently entirely intact.

Masahiko: I wasn't a minute too soon in running home. If I'd stayed any longer, I probably would have been swept away too. Like they say, when a tsunami comes, you don't go back for things, or even go after family members, but immediately strike out for high ground on your own. Everyone has to look out for themselves. Wives must flee on their own, and so must their husbands. Each must flee to high ground independently as fast as possible.

Many people were lost because they went back for something important, or went off looking for someone.

Fumiko: The hardest thing to deal with is the loss of so many friends who were fine just the day before. The shock was so great, I thought I would die myself.

They say "building something takes a lifetime, but in destruction only a moment." Truly, everything that we had built was destroyed in the blink of an eye.

Although I can't forget it, it's a scene I do not like to remember.

Masahiko: But for rebuilding, you also have to forget. There are people who cannot forget, and for that reason they cannot get over it.

March 11, 2011: More Than Survival

A sight I'd rather forget

Fumiko: When the earthquake struck, I was at our house. I was cutting pickles in the kitchen when all of a sudden a great shaking started. The shaking was so strong that it knocked the kettle off the stove, and it went on for a long time. I dashed out of the house still holding the knife.

Masahiko: I went offshore that day to collect seaweed from my farm, and I had finished harvesting and returned to my workplace at the port when the quake hit.

I immediately thought, "A tsunami's coming," so I moved a forklift that I'd just purchased to high ground. Then I went to help a fellow fisherman pull his boat out of the water, but the winch wouldn't work because the electricity was out. So we weren't able to pull the boat up.

As we were doing this, we could see the tide racing out. The water withdrew so far that we could see the seabed even in deep places. It was very creepy.

"This is awful," I thought, and immediately hurried to my home, which is on high ground.

The tsunami arrived about forty minutes after the earthquake. As it turned out, my boat and my new forklift were swept away by the receding water.

Fumiko: Our house is on high ground, so we could see the town being swallowed up by the waves. I remember

Back to the sea at Rikuzentakata, once again hoisting the "Big Catch" flag of victory!

Masahiko Murakami is a fisherman of many years, and also did sea farming of Sanriku seaweed, scallops, and rock oysters. Although many of his fishing acquaintances left the business after the great earthquake, Masahiko bought a new boat and has returned to the sea.

Masahiko Murakami

Fumiko Murakami

(Rikuzentakata City, Iwate Prefecture)

a thing have to happen?

But for just that reason, all those people will never be forgotten, be it ten years from now or twenty. Those of us who remain must live through this as much for the sake of those who died as for ourselves, and I firmly believe that doing this is a part of the mission I must fulfill.

she recovered with encouragement from many people, and now has come to understand the treasure of human connections.

My hope is that all the children who experienced the horror of "3/11" will grow and achieve happiness in their lives.

I also hope they will develop greater awareness of the importance of contributing to their home region. Nothing would make me happier than for them to become adults who can contribute to the Tohoku area.

Kazutaka determined to strive in the stead of his lost friends and acquaintances, and continues giving encouragement to individuals affected by the disaster.

Just about every week, I visit the temporary housing facilities set up for refugees and talk to them about their concerns. Those concerns seem to be changing as time passes, and I think worries about the future are looming large.

Although the road to reconstruction is faced with great difficulty, we are determined to advance a step at a time, united together through stronger mutual ties.

When I think about all those who were lost, the sadness is too deep for words. I can't help but think, why did such

Living life for lost friends

The elementary school where I worked was scheduled to be merged with two other nearby schools in 2012, but due to the earthquake, the merger was carried out following the earthquake. Since this was done in haste, during the first year the newly-merged school had three principals, three assistant principals, and three school songs, all of which had to be sung in turn (laughs).

I think being in an unfamiliar environment also made things hard for the children.

Since there were no classrooms to spare, I had to teach my special needs kids in a container for two years.

Each year, the schools in Ofunato City hold a "Sanriku Ofunato Story Contest", to which students submit stories that they have written themselves. One of the fifth grade girls from our school won first prize in that contest.

The story was about the tsunami, but was written from the point of view of a hermit crab. In the story, the hermit crab relates how "Humans were so self-centered before the earthquake, but afterwards they started giving each other encouragement. Maybe humans aren't so bad after all."

The child who wrote that lost her beloved aunt to the tsunami. For a while, the shock of loss kept her from sleeping, and she became very despondent. However,

also.

With that recent experience under their belts, the kids did not panic, and they handled the situation fairly calmly.

With Kazutaka's guidance, seventy-three students and teachers were all safely evacuated. Says Kazutaka, "The most important step in preparing for disaster is regular practice."

The tsunami arrived about thirty minutes after the earthquake. The first wave only floated some cars in the school yard, but as it started to recede, a second black flood that rose up fifteen meters arrived, entirely swallowing up the three-storey school building.

As I watched this sight from the place where we huddled on high ground, I wondered whether I was dreaming, and thought about how if this had happened while the kids were at home, many of them might have been lost to the water.

I passed the rest of that day and the following night together with the children in the public hall on high ground. Naturally, I was worried about family and friends, but there was no way I could leave that spot.

There was no electricity, and the telephones didn't work, so my total focus had to be on protecting the children.

March 11, 2011: More Than Survival

School swallowed up by the tsunami

The elementary school where I worked was located about two hundred meters from the shore of Okirai bay.

The violent shaking started just as I entered the staff room after finishing a class for special needs students. The shaking was so strong that a spiral staircase on the side of the school was torn away from the building.

The school's principal told us, "The tsunami will be coming. Let's get out of here now!!" So I ran back up to the second floor and went around the classrooms, calling to the students to evacuate to high ground.

Just the previous year, a bridge that provided direct access to high ground in the event of a major quake had been completed, so we quickly evacuated the students across that bridge.

Tsunamis over the centuries have repeatedly inflicted major damage in the area, such as those generated by the 1933 Sanriku Earthquake and the 1960 Chile Earthquake, so most schools along the coast held annual evacuation drills. Our school had its drill on March 1, just ten days before the earthquake.

Further, a fairly large earthquake that struck off the Sanriku coast on March 9 caused a tsunami of about 60 -centimeters, and we evacuated the school at that time

Protecting students' lives through daily training and disaster prevention awareness

Immediately after the earthquake, Kazutaka Yamamoto, an elementary school teacher, evacuated the students of his school and protected their lives. Telling his students, "I especially want those who have experienced loss to become happy," he continues giving them daily encouragement.

Kazutaka Yamamoto

(Ofunato City, Iwate Prefecture)

person's heart. I know we have the backing of people from all over the country, so there's no way we'll ever be defeated!

We will look forward to a shining future for Kamaishi with a song on our lips and sunshine in our hearts as we take this road of hope a step at a time.

and do something to help people." That determination is what led to his current work.

Hideo: After living in temporary housing for four years and seven months, our application for moving into reconstruction housing was selected and we moved to our new place in April, 2015.

Kyoko: Although we lost many precious things, we are happy now. While we were in temporary housing, we were blessed with fine neighbors, and when we moved into our new place we were greeted warmly there too.

What I've learned from the earthquake is the importance of building relationships on a daily basis, whether with people near or far. I think those relationships are very important in times of need.

Hideo: Although we lost our house and all our property, the words "My spirit is unbreakable" were a source of encouragement. I take them to mean, "Even when it looks like all is lost, what matters is winning in the end."

The article I clipped is one thing I kept from the tsunami, and I still treasure it.

Reconstruction of our town is going slowly, and the fishing industry has still not recovered. The future is uncertain, and I'm sure there will be difficulties, but what matters most is the recovery that takes place in each

He fell into social isolation and stayed that way for fourteen years.

Hideo: Every year when New Year's came around, I would pray, "Let this be the year that my son breaks free." I would repeat it every year, "Let this be the year." The thing that kept me going was a little mantra, "My spirit is unbreakable." I cut those words out of a magazine and kept them with me everywhere.

Kyoko: I was in agony about it too, but I think it was our son who suffered most.

And it was our son who broke out of his isolation when disaster struck. When one of his old friends came from Kanagawa to help, he went with him to an employment agency, found a job, and started working. Now he has a driver's license and is working in child support for a non-profit organization.

Hideo: The other day, he bought a used car with money that he saved.

Even though we lost our house, I think it's great that this loss motivated him to connect with other people again. More than anything, I think it was encouragement from former friends that helped. I am truly grateful.

When Tsugio saw so many people working selflessly after the earthquake, he started thinking, "I want to be like them,

the tsunami had scoured everything away, and there was not a trace left of our house. We were at loss for words.

My family home in Otsuchi was also swept away, and the body of my brother, who was carried away with the house, was found four days later. In the end, we took refuge in my sister's house.

Hideo: Because of the circumstances, some of my friends crossed the mountains from the interior to see whether we were safe. Later, they brought us rice and supplies that made all the difference. We were so grateful.

Kyoko: We could not allow ourselves to be defeated. I thought, there is nothing for it but for us to struggle through.

"My spirit is unbreakable"

Kyoko: Before the earthquake, our son would not come out of his room even to eat. I always put his meals in a lunch box and took them to him.

Just before summer vacation during his second year of high school, he said "I don't want to go to school any more." He dropped out, and started withdrawing from people. He did try working in places like izakaya and box lunch vendors, but he couldn't handle the human contact and the jobs never lasted long.

looking for a safe place. Along the way, I remembered that I had forgotten something, and wanted to turn back, but my son said "No!" That one word saved our lives.

Kyoko: I imagine many people thought Kamaishi was safe, because it had one of the greatest breakwaters in the world. A few days before the great earthquake of March 11, we had a 40-centimeter tsunami from another earthquake, and since it was no problem, I think many people had a false sense of security. That turned out to be over-confidence. When an earthquake strikes, you just have to run to the highest place you can find.

Hideo: The image I have of the 1960 tsunami from the Chile Earthquake is that it struck all in a rush, but during this tsunami, the water level seemed to rise in stages. One of our neighborhood friends said that the tsunami looked like a black dot at first, and that it made a crunching sound as it approached.

We lost eight of our neighborhood friends and acquaintances to the tsunami.

Kyoko: We spent that night in the car on a multi-function public ground, and when we tried to return to our home the next day, the road was closed. We tried walking to our house on a back street, but there was so much mud everywhere that walking was almost impossible.

We did make it as far as our neighborhood. However,

House gone without a trace

The breakwater at the mouth of Kamaishi bay was completed in March, 2009. It was a huge structure, said to be the deepest breakwater in the world. However, the force of the tsunami generated by the 2011 earthquake was so great, it overwhelmed and destroyed the breakwater. The result was catastrophic damage to the city.

Kyoko: When the shaking started, I was out of the house with my husband. I have long lived by the sea, and I was raised hearing stories of the horror of tsunamis. I was always told, "If a big earthquake strikes, run away to the highest place you can find."

But I was worried about my son, Tsugio. My son had long been socially withdrawn, and I was afraid that even an earthquake of this magnitude might not get him to leave the house. I was also worried that the house might have collapsed, and he might be buried in the rubble.

What's more, our house was located just twenty meters from the water. All I could think of was saving my son before the tsunami arrived, so we hurried home, and I was astonished to find my son standing at the entrance to the house!

Hideo: The three of us got in the car and headed off

March 11, 2011: More Than Survival

Moved by disaster, son makes comeback from fourteen years of social isolation

Although the Sugitas' home was swept away by the tsunami, the disaster helped motivate their son to break out of his social isolation. Saying, "I want to help people," he began doing welfare work.

Hideo Sugita

Kyoko Sugita

(Kamaishi City, Iwate Prefecture)

Those of us in the Youth Division who have worked on this project believe that these testimonies are proof that the "treasure of the heart" is indestructible, even in the face of a once-in-a-millennium disaster. We also believe that making them available to future generations will help pass along the treasure of that understanding.

In closing, we would like to express our appreciation to Daisanbunmei-sha, Inc. and the many people who have contributed to making this publication possible.

    March 2016
    Soka Gakkai Tohoku Youth Division

of the Youth Division participating in volunteer recovery efforts have often expressed surprise, making statements like, "These are experiences of great significance. They give me a renewed sense of the importance of fulfilling my personal mission in contributing to recovery."

On the other hand, those who shared memories of the disaster with us have said that, even though recovery is still underway, talking to someone about their experiences has helped them come to terms with their memories. Some have also said, "Putting these things in print can serve as a lesson to young people."

The importance of "sharing experiences" has been highlighted in the "Sendai Framework for Disaster Risk Reduction," a document that was adopted in March 2015 at the World Conference on Disaster Risk Reduction.

Of all the means available to keep memories from fading, the recorded recollections of those who lived through those dark days may be the most important. Such recollections also constitute powerful proof of the power of the human spirit in overcoming any difficulty.

high above the water level, while other towns remain uninhabitable.

A vague sense of restored normalcy increasingly veils the scars that linger in people's hearts.

Some of those people lost parents and children, while others lost home towns. Yet, learning what the disaster victims and refugees experienced and felt becomes increasingly difficult as time goes by.

Therefore, as part of the "SOKA Global Action" peace campaign, the Youth Division of the Tohoku Soka Gakkai launched an effort to collect accounts from people who lived through the disaster. These collected accounts are being serially published in the monthly educational periodical "Todai (Lighthouse)" under the title, "March 11 — More Than Survival: Messages to Our Children."

Now we have decided to publish a collection of representative testimonies from that series, including their translations into English.

In listening to accounts of those days' events, as well as the memories of people who lived through them, members

Publication Note

Now five years have passed since the 2011 Great East Japan Earthquake and Tsunami. Although March 11 is a turning point in history, it is not fitting to call it an anniversary, nor does it represent some sort of goal.

March 11 is a "death day" for the many people who lost their lives. The day after, March 12, is a "day of exile" for the thousands who were forced from their homes by the accident at the Fukushima Daiichi Nuclear Power Station.

We feel this keenly in the stories told by people who lived through those twin disasters.

"On that day, the happy lives we had were cruelly torn apart. We have moved many times since then, and are still living the life of refugees." There is so much we would never know without the stories told by those whose lives were affected.

If you go to the disaster zone today, you will find some towns where marks of the disaster have mostly been erased. Elsewhere, work is underway to raise entire towns

CONTENTS

Publication Note ·· 6

Hideo Sugita / Kyoko Sugita ······················ 10

Kazutaka Yamamoto ································· 17

Masahiko Murakami / Fumiko Murakami ········ 23

Kiyohide Chiba ······································· 31

Ken Matsuda ·· 40

Ken'ichi Kurosawa ·································· 48

Yoshihiro Matsumoto / Yuko Matsumoto ·········· 56

Sakae Akaishizawa / Toshiko Akaishizawa ········ 64

Kaneji Kanazawa / Kiyoko Kanazawa ············ 72

Mikio Yamane ·· 80

Copyright © Soka Gakkai 2016

Published in 2016
by Daisanbunmei-sha, Inc.
1-23-5 Shinjuku Shinjuku-ku, Tokyo Japan

http://www.daisanbunmei.co.jp

Edited by Soka Gakkai Tohoku Youth Division

Photographs by Kiyotaka Shishido
Photographs by Shigeru Bokuda (p.72)

Translated from the Japanese by Sessen International Co., Ltd. /Andrew Clark
Cover design and Page layout by Yuichi Kimura (ZERO MEGA Co., Ltd.)

All rights reserved.
No part of this text may be reproduced, transmitted,
or stored in or introduced into any information storage and retrieval system,
in any form or by any means whether electronic or mechanical,
now known or hereinafter invented,
without the express written permission of the publisher.

ISBN978-4-476-06229-8

Printed and Bound by FUJIWARA Printing Co., Ltd.

March 11, 2011
More Than Survival

Messages to the Future

DAISANBUNMEI-SHA
TOKYO

「3・11」生命の記憶
――未来へのメッセージ

2016年3月11日　初版第1刷発行

編　者	創価学会東北青年部
発行者	大島光明
発行所	株式会社　第三文明社
	東京都新宿区新宿1-23-5
	郵便番号：160-0022
	電話番号：03-5269-7154（編集代表）
	03-5269-7144（営業代表）
	03-5269-7145（注文専用ダイヤル）
	振替口座　00150-3-117823
	URL http://www.daisanbunmei.co.jp
英語翻訳	株式会社セッセン・インターナショナル
	アンドリュー・クラーク
装幀・本文DTP	木村祐一（株式会社ゼロメガ）
印刷・製本	藤原印刷株式会社

©Soka Gakkai 2016　Printed in Japan
ISBN978-4-476-06229-8

乱丁・落丁本はお取り換えいたします。ご面倒ですが、小社営業部宛にお送りください。
送料は当方で負担いたします。
法律で認められた場合を除き、本書の無断複写・複製・転載を禁じます。